"America's favorite writer."
—*The New Yorker*

❧

"Roberts is indeed a word artist,
painting her story and her characters
with vitality and verve."
—*Los Angeles Daily News*

❧

"Roberts weaves a story like no one else."
—*Rocky Mountain News*

**A story of misplaced expectations from
#1 *New York Times* bestselling author Nora Roberts.**

For a change of pace, renowned anthropologist Kasey Wyatt takes a job working for bestselling author Jordan Taylor, who needs help researching his latest novel about the Plains Indians.

Upon arriving at Jordan's impressive Palm Springs estate, Kasey finds all the trappings of a family, but none of the warmth. Jordan's forbidding mother is immediately suspicious of her, while Jordan's shy and serious orphaned niece represses her curiosity. Jordan himself is an expert at hiding his emotions behind an aristocratic facade.

Hardly the quiet and bookish woman they were all expecting, Kasey infuses their lives with light and laughter. And suddenly Jordan finds himself drawn to a woman unlike any he has ever desired, one who is able to transform his day-to-day existence into a life worth living . . .

⸎⊚⸎

"You can't bottle wish fulfillment, but Ms. Roberts certainly knows how to put it on the page."   —*The New York Times*

"When it comes to true romance, no one does it better than Nora."   —*Booklist* (starred review)

Series

Irish Born Trilogy

BORN IN FIRE
BORN IN ICE
BORN IN SHAME

Dream Trilogy

DARING TO DREAM
HOLDING THE DREAM
FINDING THE DREAM

Chesapeake Bay Saga

SEA SWEPT
RISING TIDES
INNER HARBOR
CHESAPEAKE BLUE

Gallaghers of Ardmore Trilogy

JEWELS OF THE SUN
TEARS OF THE MOON
HEART OF THE SEA

Three Sisters Island Trilogy

DANCE UPON THE AIR
HEAVEN AND EARTH
FACE THE FIRE

Key Trilogy

KEY OF LIGHT
KEY OF KNOWLEDGE
KEY OF VALOR

In the Garden Trilogy

BLUE DAHLIA
BLACK ROSE
RED LILY

Circle Trilogy

MORRIGAN'S CROSS
DANCE OF THE GODS
VALLEY OF SILENCE

Sign of Seven Trilogy

BLOOD BROTHERS
THE HOLLOW
THE PAGAN STONE

Bride Quartet

VISION IN WHITE
BED OF ROSES
SAVOR THE MOMENT
HAPPY EVER AFTER

The Inn BoonsBoro Trilogy

THE NEXT ALWAYS
THE LAST BOYFRIEND
THE PERFECT HOPE

The Cousins O'Dwyer Trilogy

DARK WITCH
SHADOW SPELL

eBooks

Cordina's Royal Family
AFFAIRE ROYALE
COMMAND PERFORMANCE
THE PLAYBOY PRINCE
CORDINA'S CROWN JEWEL

The Donovan Legacy
CAPTIVATED
ENTRANCED
CHARMED
ENCHANTED

The O'Hurleys
THE LAST HONEST WOMAN
DANCE TO THE PIPER
SKIN DEEP
WITHOUT A TRACE

Night Tales
NIGHT SHIFT
NIGHT SHADOW
NIGHTSHADE
NIGHT SMOKE
NIGHT SHIELD

The MacGregors
THE WINNING HAND
THE PERFECT NEIGHBOR
ALL THE POSSIBILITIES
ONE MAN'S ART
TEMPTING FATE
PLAYING THE ODDS
THE MACGREGOR BRIDES
THE MACGREGOR GROOMS
REBELLION / IN FROM THE COLD
FOR NOW, FOREVER

The Calhouns
COURTING CATHERINE
A MAN FOR AMANDA
FOR THE LOVE OF LILAH
SUZANNA'S SURRENDER
MEGAN'S MATE

Irish Legacy Trilogy
IRISH THOROUGHBRED
IRISH ROSE
IRISH REBEL

BEST LAID PLANS
LOVING JACK
LAWLESS

SUMMER LOVE
BOUNDARY LINES
DUAL IMAGE
FIRST IMPRESSIONS
THE LAW IS A LADY
LOCAL HERO
THIS MAGIC MOMENT
THE NAME OF THE GAME
PARTNERS
TEMPTATION
THE WELCOMING
OPPOSITES ATTRACT
TIME WAS
TIMES CHANGE
GABRIEL'S ANGEL
HOLIDAY WISHES
THE HEART'S VICTORY

THE RIGHT PATH
RULES OF THE GAME
SEARCH FOR LOVE
BLITHE IMAGES
FROM THIS DAY
SONG OF THE WEST
ISLAND OF FLOWERS
HER MOTHER'S KEEPER
UNTAMED
SULLIVAN'S WOMAN
LESS OF A STRANGER
REFLECTIONS
DANCE OF DREAMS
STORM WARNING
ONCE MORE WITH FEELING
A MATTER OF CHOICE
ENDINGS AND BEGINNINGS

Nora Roberts & J. D. Robb

REMEMBER WHEN

J. D. Robb

Anthologies

FROM THE HEART
A LITTLE MAGIC
A LITTLE FATE

MOON SHADOWS
(with Jill Gregory, Ruth Ryan Langan, and Marianne Willman)

The Once Upon Series
(with Jill Gregory, Ruth Ryan Langan, and Marianne Willman)

ONCE UPON A CASTLE
ONCE UPON A STAR
ONCE UPON A DREAM

ONCE UPON A ROSE
ONCE UPON A KISS
ONCE UPON A MIDNIGHT

SILENT NIGHT
(with Susan Plunkett, Dee Holmes, and Claire Cross)

OUT OF THIS WORLD
(with Laurell K. Hamilton, Susan Krinard, and Maggie Shayne)

BUMP IN THE NIGHT
(with Mary Blayney, Ruth Ryan Langan, and Mary Kay McComas)

DEAD OF NIGHT
(with Mary Blayney, Ruth Ryan Langan, and Mary Kay McComas)

THREE IN DEATH

SUITE 606
(with Mary Blayney, Ruth Ryan Langan, and Mary Kay McComas)

IN DEATH

THE LOST
(with Patricia Gaffney, Mary Blayney, and Ruth Ryan Langan)

THE OTHER SIDE
(with Mary Blayney, Patricia Gaffney, Ruth Ryan Langan, and Mary Kay McComas)

THE UNQUIET
(with Mary Blayney, Patricia Gaffney, Ruth Ryan Langan, and Mary Kay McComas)

MIRROR, MIRROR
(with Mary Blayney, Elaine Fox, Ruth Ryan Langan, and R. C. Ryan)

Also available . . .

THE OFFICIAL NORA ROBERTS COMPANION
(edited by Denise Little and Laura Hayden)

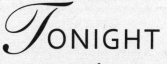

TONIGHT and ALWAYS

NORA ROBERTS

BERKLEY BOOKS, NEW YORK

THE BERKLEY PUBLISHING GROUP
Published by the Penguin Group
Penguin Group (USA) LLC
375 Hudson Street, New York, New York 10014

USA • Canada • UK • Ireland • Australia • New Zealand • India • South Africa • China

penguin.com

A Penguin Random House Company

Tonight and Always previously appeared in *From the Heart*, published by Jove Books

Library of Congress Cataloging-in-Publication Data

Roberts, Nora.
Tonight and always / Nora Roberts. — Berkley trade paperback edition.
pages cm
ISBN 978-0-425-27679-2 (paperback)
1. Authors—Fiction. 2. Women anthropologists—Fiction.
3. Man-woman relationships—Fiction. I. Title.
PS3568.O243T66 2014
813'.54—dc23
2014004160

PUBLISHING HISTORY
Berkley trade paperback edition / August 2014

PRINTED IN THE UNITED STATES OF AMERICA

10 9 8 7 6 5

Text design by Kristin del Rosario.

To my parents,
who've proven through sixty years of marriage
that love never goes out of style.
Thanks for being mine.

TONIGHT AND ALWAYS

CHAPTER ONE

T WAS DUSK, THAT STRANGE, ALMOST MYSTICAL interlude when light and dark are perfectly balanced. Within moments the soft blue would be transformed by the fiery colors of sunset. Shadows were lengthening; birds were quieting.

Kasey stood at the foot of the steps leading to the Taylor mansion. She glanced up at the massive white pillars and old rose brick with huge expanses of plate glass. Three stories. Here and there lights shone dimly through drawn drapes. There was a monied dignity about the place. Old money, inherent dignity.

Intimidating, she thought, letting her eyes roam up and

down again. But it did have a certain style. Under the cover of dusk the house looked serene.

Lifting a large brass knocker, she thudded it against the thick oak door. The noise boomed into the twilight. She smiled at the sound, then turned to watch the colors bleed slowly into the sky. Already it was more night than day. Behind her the door opened. Turning back, Kasey saw a small, dark woman dressed in a black uniform and white apron.

Just like in the movies, she decided, and smiled again. This just might be an adventure after all.

"Hello."

"Good evening, ma'am." The maid spoke politely and stood in the center of the doorway like a palace guard.

"Good evening," Kasey said, amused. "I believe Mr. Taylor's expecting me."

"Miss Wyatt?" Dubiously, the maid scanned her. She made no move to admit her. "I believe Mr. Taylor is expecting you tomorrow."

"Yes, well, I'm here tonight." Still smiling, she strode past the maid and into the main hall. "You might want to let him know I'm here," she suggested, and turned to stare at a three-tiered chandelier that dripped light onto the carpet.

Watching Kasey warily, the maid shut the door. "If you

would just wait here." She indicated a Louis XVI chair. "I'll inform Mr. Taylor of your arrival."

"Thank you." Her attention was already caught by a Rembrandt self-portrait. The maid moved soundlessly away.

Kasey studied the Rembrandt and went on to the next painting. Renoir. The place was like a museum, she decided, then continued to move idly down the hall, viewing paintings as she would in an art gallery. To Kasey, such works of art were public property—to be respected, admired, and most of all, seen. I wonder if anybody really lives here, she thought and flicked a finger over a thick gold frame.

The murmur of voices caught her attention. Instinctively, she drifted toward the sound.

"She is one of the leading authorities on American Indian culture, Jordan. Her last paper was highly acclaimed. Being only twenty-five, she's rather a phenomenon in anthropological circles."

"I'm well aware of that, Harry, or I wouldn't have agreed with your suggestion that she collaborate with me on this book." Jordan Taylor swirled a pre-dinner martini. He drank slowly, contemplatively. The drink was dry and perfect, with only a hint of vermouth. "I do find myself wondering how we're going to get on over the next few months.

Professional spinsters are intimidating, and not my favorite companions."

"You're not looking for a companion, Jordan," the other man reminded him and plucked the olive from his own glass. "You're looking for an expert on American Indian culture. That's what you're getting." He swallowed the olive. "Companions can be distracting."

With a grimace, Jordan Taylor set down his glass. He was restless without knowing why. "I hardly think I'll find your Miss Wyatt a distraction." He slipped his hands into the pockets of his perfectly tailored slacks and watched his the other man polish off the martini. "I have a composite picture: mud-colored hair scraped back from a bony face, thick glasses with three-inch lenses perched on a prominent nose. Sensible suits to accent her lack of shape, and size-ten orthopedic shoes."

"Size six."

Both men turned to the doorway and stared.

"Hello, Mr. Taylor." Kasey entered. Crossing the room, she extended her hand to Jordan. "And you must be Dr. Rhodes. We've done quite a bit of corresponding over the past weeks, haven't we? I'm glad to meet you."

"Yes, well. I . . ." Harry's thick brows lowered.

"I'm Kathleen Wyatt." She gave him a dazzling smile

before turning back to Jordan. "As you can see, I don't scrape back my hair. It probably wouldn't stay scraped back if I tried." She tugged on one of the loose curls that surrounded her face.

"And rather than mud-colored," she continued smoothly, "this shade is generally known as strawberry blond. My face isn't particularly bony, though I do have rather nice cheekbones. Have you got a light?"

She rummaged through her purse for a cigarette, then looked expectantly at Harry Rhodes. He fumbled in his pocket and found his lighter. "Thanks. Where was I? Oh, yes," she continued before either man could speak. "I do wear glasses for reading—when I can find them—but I doubt that's quite what you meant, is it? Let's see, what else can I tell you? Can I sit down? My feet are killing me." Without waiting for a reply, she chose a gold brocade chair. She paused and flicked her cigarette in a crystal ashtray. "You already know my shoe size." Sitting back in the chair, she regarded Jordan Taylor with direct green eyes.

"Well, Miss Wyatt," he said at length. "I don't know whether to apologize or applaud."

"I'd rather have a drink. Do you have any tequila?"

With a nod, he moved to the bar. "I don't believe we do; would vermouth do?"

"That would do fine, thank you."

Kasey surveyed the room. It was large and perfectly square with rich paneling and heavily brocaded furnishings. An intricately carved marble fireplace dominated one wall. Dresden porcelain reflected in a wide, mahogany-framed mirror above it. The carpet was thick, the drapes heavy.

Too formal, she thought, observing the structured elegance. She would have preferred the drapes opened wide, or better yet, removed completely and replaced with something a bit less somber. There was probably a beautiful hardwood floor under the carpeting.

"Miss Wyatt." Jordan brought her attention back to him as he handed her a glass. Each one curious about the other, their eyes met, then a movement in the doorway distracted their attention.

"Jordan, Millicent tells me that Miss Wyatt has arrived, but she must have wandered— Oh." The woman who'd glided into the room halted as she spotted Kasey. "You're Kathleen Wyatt?" With the same wariness the maid had shown, she surveyed the woman dressed in gray trousers and a brilliant peacock blue blouse.

Kasey sipped and smiled. "Yes, I am." She made her own survey of the elegant society matron. Jordan Taylor's mother, Beatrice Taylor, was carefully made up, impeccably groomed and stylishly attired. Beatrice Taylor knew who and what she was, Kasey thought.

"You must forgive the confusion, Miss Wyatt. We weren't expecting you until sometime tomorrow."

"I got things organized more quickly than I expected," Kasey said, and sipped at her drink. "I caught an earlier flight." She smiled again. "I didn't see any point in wasting time."

"Of course." Beatrice's face creased for a moment in a frown. "Your room's prepared." She turned her eyes to her son. "I've put Miss Wyatt in the Regency Room."

"Adjoining Alison?" Jordan paused in the act of lighting a thin cigar and glanced at his mother.

"Yes, I thought perhaps Miss Wyatt would enjoy the company. Alison is my granddaughter," she explained to Kasey. "She's been with us since my son and his wife were killed three years ago. She was only eight, poor dear." Her attention shifted back to Jordan. "If you'll excuse me, I'll see about Miss Wyatt's bags."

"Well." Jordan took a seat on the sofa when his mother slipped from the room. "Perhaps we should discuss business for a moment."

"Of course." Kasey finished off the vermouth and set the glass on the table beside her. "Do you like a strict routine—

7

you know, designated hours? Nine to two, eight to ten. Or do you just like to flow?"

"Flow?" Jordan repeated and glanced up at Harry.

"You know. Flow." She made a descriptive gesture with her hands.

"Ah, flow." Jordan nodded, amused. This was definitely not the straightlaced, low-key scientist of his imagination. "Why don't we try a little of both?"

"Good. I'd like to go over your outline tomorrow and get a better feel for what you have in mind. You can let me know what you want to concentrate on first."

Kasey studied Jordan for a moment as Harry fixed himself another martini. Very attractive, she decided, in a smooth, Wall Street sort of manner. Nice hair; warm brown with just a few light touches. He must get out of this museum now and then to get sun-streaked, she thought, but she doubted whether he was much of a beachcomber. She had always liked blue eyes in a man, and Jordan's were very dark. And, she thought, very shrewd. A lean face. Good bones. She wondered if he had any Cheyenne blood in him. The skull structure was very similar. The sophisticated clothes and manners were offset by a certain sensuousness around the mouth. She liked the contrast. He was built like a tennis player, she mused. Good shoulders, trim, strong hands. His tailor was obviously exclusive and conservative. Too bad, she thought.

But watch out, she told herself, there's a bit more here than meets the eye. She had a feeling there was a temper under the cool sophistication. She knew, from reading his books, that he was intelligent. The only fault she had found with his work was a certain coldness.

"I'm sure we'll work very well together, Mr. Taylor," she said aloud. "I'm looking forward to getting started. You're a fine writer."

"Thank you."

"Don't thank me, I didn't have anything to do with it." She smiled.

Jordan's lips curved in instinctive response even as he wondered what he had gotten himself into.

"I'm very pleased to have the opportunity to help you with your research," she went on. "I suppose I really should thank you, Dr. Rhodes, for suggesting my name." Her gaze shifted and locked on Harry.

"Well, you, ah—your credentials—were impeccable," Harry stammered as he tried to connect the Kathleen Wyatt whose papers he had read with the slim, curly-haired whirlwind who was smiling at him. "You graduated magna cum laude from University of Maryland?"

"That's right. I majored in anthropology at Maryland, then took my masters at Columbia. I worked with Dr. Spalding on his Colorado expedition. I believe it was my paper on that which brought me to your attention."

"Excuse me, sir." The dark maid hovered in the doorway. "Miss Wyatt's baggage has been taken to her room. Mrs. Taylor suggested that perhaps she would like to freshen up before dinner."

"I'll skip dinner, thanks." Kasey spoke to the maid directly, then turned back to Dr. Rhodes. "I will go up, though. Traveling tires me out. Good night, Dr. Rhodes. I suppose we'll be seeing each other over the next few months. I'll see you in the morning, Mr. Taylor."

She swept out as she had swept in, leaving both men staring after her.

"Well, Harry." Jordan thought he could all but feel the room settle back into order. "What was it you were saying about distractions?"

After following the maid up the stairs, Kasey stood in the doorway of her room. Pale pinks and golds dominated the color scheme. Pink drapes hung against oyster white walls; pink and gold cushions graced ornately carved Regency chairs. There was a gold skirted vanity table and a large, plush-covered lounge in a deeper shade of rose. The bed was huge and canopied, complete with bed-curtains and a pink satin spread.

"Good grief," she murmured and stepped across the threshold.

"I beg your pardon, miss?"

Kasey turned to the maid and smiled. "Nothing. This is quite a room."

"The bath is through here, Miss Wyatt. Would you care to have me draw you one now?"

"Draw my— No." Kasey grinned, unable to do otherwise. "No, thank you—Millicent, right?"

"Yes, miss. Very well, miss. If you require anything, just press nine on the house phone." Millicent slipped noiselessly out the door, closing it carefully behind her.

Kasey dropped her purse on the bed and began to explore the room.

To her mind, it was entirely too proper and pink. She decided she would ignore it and spend as little time within its walls as possible. Besides, she was too tired from planes and taxis to care where she slept now. She began to search for the nightgown that Millicent had apparently tucked away in a bureau.

"Come on in," she called as a knock sounded on the door. She continued to rummage through the carefully folded lingerie. She lifted her eyes to the mirror. "Hello. You must be Alison."

She saw a tall, thin child in a simply cut, expensive dress. Her long blond hair was carefully groomed, pulled neatly back with a headband. Her eyes were large and dark, but their expression was neither happy nor unhappy. Kasey felt a stirring of pity.

"Good evening, Miss Wyatt." Alison broke the silence but came no farther into the room. "I thought I should introduce myself, as we'll be sharing a bath for the next few months."

"Good idea." Kasey turned from the mirror and faced Alison directly. "Though I imagine we'd have run across each other in the shower before too long."

"If you have a preference for your bath time, Miss Wyatt, I would be happy to accommodate you."

Kasey moved to the bed to drop her nightgown. "I'm not fussy. I've shared bathrooms before." She sat gingerly on the edge of the bed and glanced up dubiously at the canopy. "I'll try to stay out of your way in the mornings. You go to school, I imagine."

"Yes, I'm attending school this year. Last year I had a tutor. I'm very high-strung."

"Is that so?" Kasey lifted her brows and struggled with a smile. "I'm low-strung, myself."

Alison frowned at this. Unable to decide whether to advance or retreat, she hesitated on the threshold.

Kasey noted the uncertainty, the trained manners, the hands that were neatly folded at the waist of the expensive dress. She remembered the child was only eleven. "Tell me, Alison, what do you do around here for fun?"

"Fun?" Fascinated, Alison stepped into the room.

"Yes, fun. You can't go to school all the time." She pushed a stray curl out of her eyes. "And I'm definitely not going to be working twenty-four hours a day."

"There's a tennis court." Alison came a bit closer. "And the pool, of course."

Kasey nodded. "I like to swim." She went on before Alison could comment, "But I'm not too good at tennis. Do you play?"

"Yes, I—"

"Terrific. Maybe you can give me some lessons." Her eyes swept the room again. "Tell me, is your room pink?"

Alison stared a moment, trying to understand the change in topic. "No, it's done in blues and greens."

"Hmmm, good choice." Kasey made a face at the drapes. "I painted my room purple once when I was fifteen. I had nightmares for two months." She caught Alison's unblinking stare. "Something wrong?"

"You don't look like an anthropologist," Alison blurted out, then caught her breath at her lack of manners.

"No?" Kasey thought of Jordan and lifted her brows. "Why?"

"You're pretty." A blush rushed into Alison's cheeks.

"You think so?" Kasey rose to peer at herself in the mirror. She narrowed her eyes. "Sometimes I think so, but mostly I think my nose is too small."

Alison was staring at Kasey's reflection. As their eyes met in the glass, Kasey's lit with a smile. It was slow, warm and all-encompassing. Alison's lips, so much like her uncle's, curved in unconscious response.

"I have to go down to dinner now." She backed out of the door, unwilling to lose sight of the smile. "Good night, Miss Wyatt."

"Good night, Alison."

Turning as the door shut, Kasey sighed. An interesting group, she decided. Her mind turned toward Jordan again. Very interesting.

She walked over and picked up the nightgown again, then ran it idly through her hands. And where, she wondered, does Kasey Wyatt fit into all of this? With a sigh, she sat on the lounge chair. The conversation between Jordan and Dr. Rhodes that she had walked in on had been more amusing than annoying. But still . . . Kasey let Jordan's description of her run through her mind again.

Typical, she decided. A typical layman's view of a scientist who happens to be a woman. Kasey was perfectly aware that she had unsettled Harry Rhodes. A smile tugged at her mouth. She thought she would like him. He was rather staid and pompous and, she reflected, probably very sweet. Beatrice Taylor was another matter. Kasey leaned back in the lounge chair and ordered herself to relax. There would be no common ground between herself and the older woman, but, Kasey thought, if they were lucky, there would be no animosity. As for the child . . .

Alison. Mature for her age—maybe too mature. Kasey knew what it was like to lose parents in childhood. There were feelings of confusion, betrayal, guilt. It was a lot for a young person to cope with. Kasey closed her eyes and began to unbutton her blouse as she lay there. Who mothers her now? she wondered. Beatrice? Kasey shook her head. Somehow, she couldn't picture the elegant matron mothering an eleven-year-old girl. She would see that Alison was well-dressed, well-fed, and well-mannered. Kasey felt a second stir of pity.

Then there was Jordan. With another sigh, Kasey roused herself enough to pull off her blouse and slip off her shoes.

He wouldn't be an easy man to get close to. Kasey wasn't at all certain she wanted to.

Standing, she unbuckled her trousers and headed for the bath. What she wanted was to put her education and her experience to work on his book. She wanted to see the information she gave him utilized in the best possible manner. What she wanted, she thought and turned the hot water on full, was a bath. The hours on the plane, preceded by a week of lecturing in New York, had left her as close to exhaustion as she ever came. Thinking of Jordan Taylor would simply have to wait.

Tomorrow, she thought as she lowered herself into the tub, would be here soon enough.

CHAPTER TWO

THE SUN GLITTERED OVER THE POOL'S SURFACE AS Jordan completed his tenth lap. He cut through the water with strong, sure strokes. When he swam, he didn't think but simply let his body take over. As a novelist, he found his mind too often crowded with characters, with places. With words. He started off the day by clearing it with something physical.

That morning there had been one more character intruding into his brain. Kathleen Wyatt. He had found her fascinating. He wasn't at all certain he wanted to be fascinated by a collaborator. His work was important to him, and the novel he was currently working on might be the most important in his career. He thought perhaps it would have been better if Kathleen Wyatt had been closer to the woman of his imagination. The reality of her was entirely too unsettling.

As he reached the pool edge and made to turn for another lap, a movement caught his attention. Jordan glanced up to see a vague face surrounded by red-gold curls.

"Hi."

Shaking water from his eyes, Jordan narrowed them against the sun. He focused on his collaborator. Kasey sat cross-legged at the pool's edge. Her cutoffs and T-shirt exposed skin still pale from October in New York. Her eyes were bright with amusement as she smiled at him. Entirely too unsettling, he thought again.

"Good morning, Miss Wyatt. You're up early."

"I suppose I haven't adjusted to the time change." Her voice, he realized all at once, wasn't eastern but had the slightest hint of the south. "I went for a run."

"A run?" he repeated, distracted from trying to place the vague accent.

"Yes, I'm into running." She lifted her face and studied the perfect sky. "Actually, I was into running before it was something to get into. Even though I resent being part of a trend, I can't stop. Do you swim every morning?"

"Whenever I can."

"Maybe I'll try that instead. Swimming uses more muscles, and you don't sweat."

"I never thought about it quite that way." After pulling himself from the water, he reached for a towel.

Kasey watched as he briskly rubbed his hair. His body, glistening with droplets of water, was lean and hard and brown. There were ropings of muscles in his arms and shoulders. The hair on his chest was blond, like the lighter streaks on his head that the sun had bleached. The brief suit clung to his hips. Kasey discovered she had been right about the athletic body beneath the conservative suit. She felt a flutter of desire and ignored it. This was not a man to become involved with, and now was not the time.

"Swimming's certainly kept you in shape," she observed.

He paused for a moment. "Thank you, Miss Wyatt." He shook his head and picked up a short terry robe.

Kasey stood in one swift, fluid motion. Her head was level with his chin. "Would you like to get started after breakfast? If you've something else to do, I can just go over your outline and notes myself."

"No, I'd like very much to get started. The idea of picking your brain becomes more intriguing by the minute."

"Really?" Her smile flashed over her face. "I hope you won't be disappointed, Jordan. I'm going to call you Jordan now. We'd have gotten to it sooner or later."

He nodded in agreement. "Do I call you Kathleen?"

"I certainly hope not." She grinned. "No one else does."

It took him a moment to understand. "Kasey, then."

He was looking at her again in that deep, searching manner that left her slightly disconcerted. Jordan watched a frown come and go in her eyes.

"Can we eat?" she demanded. It would be simpler, she decided, if they got down to more practical matters. "I've been hungry for hours."

⌖

KASEY AND JORDAN CLOSED THEMSELVES IN THE STUDY immediately after breakfast. The room was large, its walls lined with books. Here a scent of old leather and new polish mixed with tobacco. Kasey much preferred it to the other parts of the house she had seen. Here she could detect signs of production, though it was scrupulously organized production. There were no scattered papers, no precariously piled books.

Large, dark-framed glasses perched on her nose, Kasey

sat by the window reading Jordan's notes. Her feet were bare, and one swung idly in the air as she scanned the pages.

She wasn't beautiful, Jordan decided. Not in the classic sense, at any rate. But her face was arresting. When she smiled, it seemed she lit from the inside out. Her eyes seemed to hold some private joke. She was tall and boyishly slim, narrow-hipped and long-legged. A man, he thought, would find angles rather than curves when he got into her bed. He frowned, annoyed with the turn of his mind.

There was a coltishness in her moves—an excitement and vibrancy that raced through her conversation as well. Now it was as though she had turned down the power. She was silent. Her features were tranquil. Her only movement was the carelessly swinging bare foot.

Kasey had been perfectly aware of Jordan's survey. "You have a fascinating story in the works here," she said, rupturing the silence and the sudden hum of sexual tension that had begun between them.

"Thank you." He cocked a brow. He had felt the tension, too, and was as wary of it as she.

Pulling up her legs, Kasey picked up a cigarette. She held it absently while she continued to meet his eyes. "It would seem you're dealing mainly with the Plains Indian. They do seem to most typify our image of the American Indian, though they're the least typical of all."

"Are they?" He rose to light the cigarette she still held between her fingers. "I leave it to you to clear up the misconception and give me an accurate picture."

"You could do the same with a few well-selected reference books." She settled in the chair. "Why do you need me?"

Sitting back, he gave her a considering look. His eyes made a slow, complete survey. It was calculated to disconcert.

"You didn't have to send to New York for that, either," she commented dryly. "You're not going to get maidenly blushes, Jordan." She smiled and watched his lips curve in response. "I'll tell you what," she decided on impulse. "I'll put an end to your curiosity, then you put an end to mine. I'm a professional anthropologist, not a professional virgin. Now, what, precisely, do you want from me as regards your current novel?"

"Are you always so frank?"

"Not always," she said evasively. It wouldn't be smart to get too frank with him. "Now, about your book."

"Facts; details on customs, clothing, village life; when, where and how." He paused and lit a thin cigar, then regarded Kasey through a screen of smoke. "Those are things I can get from reference books. But I want more. I want *why*."

Kasey crushed out the cigarette he had lit for her. Jordan noted that she had taken no more than two halfhearted puffs. There were more nerves in her than she let show.

"You want me to supply you with theories as to why a culture developed a certain way and why it survived or succumbed to outside pressures."

"Exactly."

With the story line he was developing and the right slant, it could be a marvelous book, Kasey thought.

"Okay," she said suddenly. With a flashing smile, she dropped her eyes to Jordan's. "I'll give you a general outline. We can pick up specifics as we move along."

⌘

THREE HOURS LATER JORDAN STOOD AT HIS WINDOW and gazed down at the pool. Kasey swam alone. She wore a one-piece suit that clung to her. He watched her dive beneath the surface and streak along the mosaic bottom.

She swam, he decided, as she did everything else—with quick bursts of energy interspersed with moments of calm. She was a sprinter, not a long-distance runner.

Kasey surfaced, rolled to her back, then floated. She

thought about Jordan Taylor as she watched a few stringy white clouds work their way across the sky. *He's brilliant, conservative, successful. Incredibly sexy. Why does that worry me?* She narrowed her eyes against the sun and let her mind and body drift. *I should be very pleased with myself to have been asked to work with him. I was. It's probably the house,* she decided and closed her eyes completely. *There's no dust in it. How do people live without dust?*

He must belong to some very exclusive country club. I imagine there are some very classy women in his life. Kasey swore at herself and rolled over.

She must have men in her life, Jordan thought. *Other scientists, professors, probably a struggling artist or two.* He cursed at himself and turned away from the window.

Kasey pulled herself from the pool and shook the water from her hair. *Well,* she thought and glanced at a lounge chair, *if I'm going to live with the wealthy for a while, I might as well enjoy it.* She flopped down and let the sun bake the chill from her damp skin. *There was something to be said for all this. Private pool, private tennis court.* She let her gaze sweep the huge expanse of lawn bordered by lush, green hedges and a stone wall. She wrinkled her nose. *Privacy we've got. I wonder how often he gets out of here.* Her mind settled back on Jordan. With a sigh, Kasey accepted the fact that he would probably continue to intrude in her thoughts. Closing her eyes, she gave in to jet lag and slept.

⚭⚭

"YOU COULD BROIL OUT HERE."

Kasey opened her eyes slowly and focused. "Hi." She gave Jordan a sleepy smile.

"You're very fair. You'll burn easily."

The hint of annoyance in his voice registered, and she studied him. "You're right, I suppose." She tested her skin by pressing a finger against her shoulder. "Not yet." She gave him another direct look. "Is something wrong?"

"No." He didn't want to admit, even to himself, that he had had a difficult time concentrating on his work knowing she was there within view of his window.

"I'll be a bit more up to standard tomorrow," she told him, thinking perhaps he was irritated that she had given him only a few hours. "Planes wear me out. It must be the altitude." Her hair was almost dry, and she pushed a hand through it absently. It appeared almost copper in the sunlight. "Do you want me?"

He looked at her thoughtfully. "Yes, I believe I do."

Kasey caught the double entendre and thought it wise to stand up. "I don't think we meant the same thing." She smiled but kept out of reach.

He took a step toward her, surprising both of them. On impulse, he reached out to touch her hair. "You're a very attractive woman."

"And you're a very attractive man," she said smoothly. "And we're going to be working in close quarters for some time. I don't think we should—complicate things. I'm not being coy, Jordan. I'm being practical. I very much want to see this book through. It could mean every bit as much to me as it will to you."

"We'll make love sooner or later, you know."

"Oh, really?" She tilted her head.

"Yes, really." Turning, he left her alone by the pool.

Well, she thought, placing her hands on her hips. Is that so? I suppose he always gets his way. She stretched out on the lounger again. Though his high-handedness irritated her, Kasey admired his directness. He could drop the polished manners and elegance when he chose to. He might be more difficult than she had anticipated.

It would be foolish to deny she was attracted to him and equally foolish to act on the attraction. Kasey frowned and twisted a curl around her finger. What did Kathleen Wyatt have in common with Jordan Taylor? Nothing. She would not, could not, involve herself emotionally or physically with a man unless there was a firm base. Attraction wasn't enough, nor was respect. There was a need for affection, for friendship. Kasey wasn't at all certain she could be friends with Jordan Taylor. Time would tell, she told herself and settled back again. Then a movement caught her eye.

Looking over, Kasey smiled and raised her hand in a wave. Alison seemed to hesitate for a moment, then walked over to join her.

"Hi, Alison. Did you just get out of school?"

"Yes, I just got home."

"I'm playing hooky." Kasey leaned back against the cushions again. "Ever played hooky?"

Alison looked horrified. "No, of course not."

"Too bad, it can be fun." A sweet child, Kasey thought, and much too lonely. She shot the young girl a grin. "What are you studying?"

"American poets."

"Have a favorite?"

"I like Robert Frost."

"I always liked Frost." Kasey smiled as lines flitted through her mind. "His poems always remind me of my grandfather."

"Your grandfather?"

"He's a doctor in a remote section of West Virginia. Blue mountains, forest, streams. Last time I went home, he was still making house calls." He'll be making them when he's a hundred, she thought, and missed him suddenly, acutely. It had been too long since she'd been home. "He's an incredible man—big and strapping with white hair and a big, booming voice. Gentle hands."

"It would be nice to have a grandfather," Alison murmured, trying to picture him. "Did you see him often when you were growing up?"

"Every day." Kasey recognized the wistfulness. She reached out to touch Alison's hair. "My parents were killed when I was eight. He raised me."

Alison's eyes were very intense. "Did you miss them?"

"Sometimes I still do." She's still hurting, Kasey thought. I wonder if any of them know it. "To me, they'll always be young and happy together. It makes it easier."

"They used to laugh," Alison murmured. "I can remember them laughing."

"That's a good memory. You'll always have it." There's not enough laughter here, Kasey decided, and felt a quick flash of anger at Jordan. Not nearly enough. "Alison." She broke into the child's thoughts. "I bet you dress for dinner."

"Yes, ma'am."

"Please." Kasey grinned and shook her head. "Don't call me that. It makes me feel a million years old. Call me Kasey."

"Grandmother wouldn't approve if I called an adult by her first name."

"Call me Kasey anyway and I'll deal with your grandmother if necessary. Why don't you come up and help me find something to wear? I don't want to disgrace the Taylor name."

Alison stared at her. "You want me to help you pick out a dress?"

"You probably know more about it than I do." Kasey smiled as she tucked Alison's arm in hers.

⤨⥱

A FEW HOURS LATER KASEY STOOD AT THE DOORWAY OF the drawing room, observing its occupants.

Beatrice Taylor sat in the gold brocade chair. She wore black silk and diamonds. Jewels glittered at her ears and throat. Alison was at the piano, dutifully practicing a selection from Brahms. Jordan stood at the bar mixing a batch of pre-dinner martinis.

The family hour. Kasey grimaced. She thought of the dinners she had shared with her grandfather—the laughter, the arguments. She thought of the noisy meals at college, with conversations ranging from the intellectual to the bizarre. She thought of the often inedible meals on various digs. Did money box you in this way? she wondered. Or was it a matter of choice?

Kasey waited until Alison had struggled through the last notes before entering the room. "Hi. You know, a person could wander around this place for days and not see another living soul."

"Miss Wyatt. You had only to ring for one of the staff. You would have been directed to the drawing room."

"Oh, that's all right. I finally made it. I hope I'm not late."

"Not at all," Jordan said. "I have only just begun to make a cocktail. How about a martini? Or perhaps you'll tell me what you want done with this tequila?"

"You got some?" Smiling, she moved to join him. "That was a nice thing to do. May I fix it?" She took the bottle from Jordan. "Watch carefully. I'm about to trust you with an old, closely guarded secret."

"Kasey's grandfather is a doctor," Alison announced suddenly. Beatrice shifted her attention from the couple at the bar to her granddaughter.

"Who is Kasey, dear?" Her tone was mildly annoyed. "One of your friends at school?"

Kasey glanced over to see Alison blush. "I'm Kasey, Mrs. Taylor," she answered easily. "You have to give it a good squeeze of lemon," she told Jordan and demonstrated. "I asked Alison to call me by my first name, Mrs. Taylor. Are you going to have one of these, Jordan?" She poured two glasses without waiting for his answer. She smiled at Beatrice, sipped, then turned back to Jordan. "What do you think?" she asked him. "Has a nice kick, doesn't it?"

He sipped, watching her. "Delicious," he murmured. "And unexpected."

She gave a quiet laugh, knowing he spoke of her and not the drink.

He found himself once more having to control the desire to touch her hair. "Don't you like knowing where your life's leading?"

"Oh, good grief, no!" she said immediately. "I want to be surprised. Don't you like surprises, Jordan?"

"I'm not at all sure," he murmured. He touched the rim of his glass to hers. "To the unexpected, then. For the time being."

Kasey wasn't at all certain what she was agreeing to, but she lifted her glass. "For the time being," she repeated.

⋙⋘

OVER THE FOLLOWING DAYS JORDAN RESIGNED HIMSELF to working seriously with Kasey. Harry had been right about one thing: She was unquestionably an expert in her field. She was also unsettling. There was a vibrant sexuality about her that she did nothing to accentuate. She rarely wore anything but the most casual of clothes and almost never bothered with even the most basic cosmetics.

He watched her as she sat on the windowsill in his study. The sun streamed onto her hair. It was Titian in this light. She wore running shorts and was again without shoes. On the third finger of her right hand she wore a very thin gold band. He had noticed it before and wondered who had given it to her and why. He doubted she would buy jewelry of any kind for herself. She wouldn't think of it.

With an effort, he pulled himself away from the woman and concentrated on her words.

"The sun dance was important to the ceremonial life of many of the Plains tribes." She had a quiet, low-key voice when she spoke like this. "Some practiced self-torture to induce trances and to aid in receiving visions. The dancer would thrust sharpened sticks through the folds of the flesh on his chest and attach the sticks to a post. He would dance, sing, and pray for a vision until he tore himself free. It was also a sign of courage and endurance. A warrior had to prove himself—to himself and to his tribe. It was their way."

"You approve?"

She shot him a look that was both amused and patient. "It's not my place to approve or disapprove. I study. I observe. As a writer, I suppose you have a different viewpoint. But if you're going to write about it, you'd better try to understand the motivations." Pushing a couple of books out of her way, she sat on the table. "If a man could endure that kind of pain, self-inflicted pain, wouldn't he be fearless in battle? Ruthless? The survival of the tribe was the first priority."

"Cultural necessity," he said and nodded. "Yes, I see what you mean."

"Visions and dreams were an essential part of their culture. Men who had strong visions often became shamans." Turning, she began rummaging through the books on the desk. "There's a rather good picture . . . Blackfoot tribe . . . if I can remember which book."

"You're left-handed," he observed.

"*Hmm?* No, actually, I'm ambidextrous."

"That could account for it," he said wryly.

"For what?" she asked, raising an eyebrow.

"For the unexpected."

Kasey laughed. Her laughter touched off something inside him. "You should do that more often."

"Do what?"

"Laugh. You have a wonderful laugh."

He was still smiling, and it pulled at her. For days, she had been able to keep her feelings regulated. Picking up a cigarette, she searched for matches. "Of course, if we laugh too much in here, your mother's going to camp on the threshold."

He watched her pushing through books and papers. "Why would she do that?"

"Come on, Jordan. You know she thinks I plan to seduce you and abscond with half your fortune. Do you have a light?"

"You're not interested in either project?"

"We're business associates," she said curtly. She moved over to the desk, still searching for matches. She could feel the lightest flutter of nerves beginning. She sought to settle them before they grew. "And though you're very attractive, the money is a strike against you."

"Is that so?" Jordan rose and joined her. "Why? People are normally attracted to money."

Hearing the annoyance, Kasey sighed and turned to face him. She thought it best for both of them if she made her position perfectly clear. "Normality is relative, Jordan."

"So speaks the anthropologist."

"Your eyes get very dark when you're angry; did you

know that? Money is very nice, Jordan. I often use it myself. But it tends to cloud reality."

"Whose reality?"

"My point exactly." She leaned back on the desk. "People with your kind of money never really see life as it is for the majority—day-to-day struggles, budgets, creditors, coupon clipping. You're removed from all that."

"You see that as a defect?"

"I didn't say that."

"Not your place to approve or disapprove?"

She blew the curls out of her eyes. How had she gotten into all this? "I'll admit it makes me nervous, but that's a personal problem. Don't you think that money tends to iso-late the individual from everyday emotions?"

"All right." He pulled her against him. "Let's test your theory."

His mouth came to hers. It was not the kiss she had expected from him. It was hungry and possessive and demanded a com-plete, unquestioned response. For a moment she resisted it. Her mind was set firmly against surrendering. But her body began to heat. She heard herself moan as she drew him closer.

There was something almost savage in the way his mouth took hers. There was no gentleness, no seduction. He sought her response, thrived on it and demanded more. She gave. Her own needs left her no choice.

His lips left hers a moment, and she drew back, trying to clear her thoughts. "Oh, no." He kept her tight against him. "Not yet. I'm not nearly finished yet."

He exploited, he ravaged, he possessed. He was pulling something from her that she was not yet ready to give. She wanted to regain herself, break free, but her arms were around him. Her mouth was determined to have more.

His hand was rough when he took her breast. His fingers were long and lean and made her skin burn at the touch. It was more than pleasure, more than passion. Those she had felt before. Here was something beyond her experience. It frightened her, made her ache, made her answer his demand with more fervor. Then, when she knew the border of sanity would be crossed, he released her.

She stared up at him. Thoughts and emotions shuddered through her. She could still feel the needs. His flavor still lingered on her lips.

"This is the first time I've seen you at a loss for words," Jordan murmured. He slipped his hand around the back of her neck. His fingers caressed. Kasey felt a new surge of desire shoot through her.

"You took me by surprise." She slid out of his grasp and

moved away from him. She was going to have to give this a great deal of thought, but now wasn't the time. She needed to find her balance again.

He watched her. It pleased him to note that he had unsettled her. But then, she had unsettled him as well. He hadn't been prepared for the intensity of the desire he had felt at the first taste of her.

"I'll have to make a habit of surprising you."

She turned and faced him. "I don't surprise easily, Jordan. And I don't plan to have an affair with you."

"Good. That should make things more interesting. I plan to have one with you."

I miscalculated, she thought to herself. He isn't as bound by social conventions as I thought. There is a strong ruthlessness under that social veneer. She would have to be more careful. She forced her voice to sound calm as she asked, "Wasn't I about to show you a picture of a shaman?"

He took the book from her hand and closed it firmly. "First things first. How would you like to take tomorrow off and go sailing?"

"Sailing?" Her tone was wary. "Just you and me?"

"That's what I had in mind."

The offer of freedom after days of being stifled in the house—the chance to be with him away from the work—

was tempting. Too tempting. She shook her head. "I don't think it would be wise."

"You don't strike me as a woman who always does what's wise." His hand slipped up over her cheek and into her hair.

"I'm making an exception. I really wish you wouldn't do that." She could feel her pulse beginning to hammer.

He kissed her gently on the temple. "Come with me, Kasey. I need a day away from this room, away from these books."

Perhaps just this once, she thought.

∽᠗᠖∾

THE BOAT WAS EVERYTHING SHE HAD EXPECTED: SLEEK, luxurious, and expensive. It had pleased her to watch Jordan handle the fifteen-foot sailing yacht with an ease that spoke of long experience. She sat at the bow so she could watch the boat slice through the ocean. This is his escape when that world he's locked himself into becomes too much for him, she mused.

Kasey watched him at the tiller. He was stripped to the waist. There was power in his arms and in his eyes. What would it be like to make love with him? She curled her legs under her on the padded bench and studied him carefully. He had marvelous hands. Even as she sat with the wind whipping around her, she could feel the touch. He would be a demanding lover, she decided, remembering the aggression of his kiss. Exciting. But . . . there's a *but*, and I'm not sure yet why it's there. I'm not sure I want to know.

Jordan looked over and caught her eye. "What are you thinking?"

"Just working out a hypothetical problem," she said, coloring. "Oh, look!" Over his shoulder she could see a school of dolphins. They leaped and dove and leaped again. "Aren't they marvelous?" She uncurled herself to go to the stern. She balanced herself by putting her hand on his shoulder, then leaned farther out. "If I were a mermaid, I'd swim with them."

"Do you believe in mermaids, Kasey?"

"Of course." She smiled at him now. "Don't you?"

"Is this the scientist asking the question?" He lifted a hand to her hip.

"Next you'll be telling me there's no Santa Claus. For a writer, you have a faulty imagination." She took a deep breath of sea air. She started to move aside, but he caught her arm. The boat listed a bit, and his fingers tightened to hold her steady. Keep it light, she told herself, trying not to respond to his touch. "You can think about it over lunch."

"Hungry?" He smiled and rose. His hands moved up her sides to rest on her shoulders.

"I usually am. I'd like to see what Francois packed in that hamper."

"In a minute." He lowered his mouth to taste hers.

It was a different sort of kiss than they had shared the day before. His lips were still confident, but today they were gentle, slower. She could feel the heat from the sun, the ribbons of wind as they whipped around her. The scent of salt was in the air. Over their heads the sails flapped and billowed.

She was losing herself again. This wasn't what she wanted, this loss of power. Very carefully she drew herself out of his arms. "Jordan," she began, then blew out a breath to steady herself. He was smiling at her, and the hands on her shoulders lightened to a caress. "You're very pleased with yourself, aren't you?" she observed.

"As a matter of fact, I am."

He turned away and remained busy for some moments dropping sail. Kasey leaned against the rail without offering assistance. "Jordan, perhaps I've given you the wrong impression." Her tone was lighter again, more at ease. "I told you I wasn't a professional virgin. But I don't go to bed with just anybody."

He didn't even glance at her. "I'm not just anybody."

She tossed back her hair. "You don't have an ego problem, do you?"

"Not that I've noticed. Where did you get that ring you wear?"

Kasey glanced down at her hand. "It was my mother's. Why?"

"Just curious." He picked up the hamper. "Shall we see now what Francois has packed for us?"

CHAPTER THREE

THE DAYS WERE GREEN AND GOLDEN IN THE PERPET-
ual summer of Palm Springs. The sky was cloudless,
the desert air dry and warm. To Kasey, the sameness was
both inescapable and stifling. Routines were a necessary part
of life that she characteristically rebelled against. The Taylor
household moved smoothly—too smoothly. There were no
curves to negotiate, no bumps. If anything could make
Kasey nervous, it was a perfection of organization. The
human condition included flaws. These Kasey understood
and accepted. But flaws were scarce in the Taylor residence.

She worked with Jordan daily, and though she was aware
that her lack of regimentation frustrated him, she was confident he could find no fault with her information. Kasey

knew her field. She learned more of him. He was an exacting, disciplined writer and a demanding, meticulous man. He was able to extrapolate precisely what he wanted from the flood of facts and theories she provided. And Kasey, a tough critic, grew to respect and admire his mind. It was simpler for her to focus on his intelligence and talent than to dwell on him as a man, an individual who both attracted and unsettled her. Kasey wasn't accustomed to being unsettled.

She wasn't at all certain she liked him. They were opposites in many ways. He was pragmatic, she voluble. He was reserved, she extroverted. He ran on intellect, Kasey ran on emotion. Both, however, were used to being in control. It disturbed her that she was not able to master her attraction for him.

Kasey would never have considered herself idealistic. Yet she had always thought that when she became deeply involved with a man, it would be with someone who would fit neatly into the packet of her requirements. He would be strong, intelligent, with a well of emotions she could easily tap. They would understand each other. She was quite certain Jordan didn't understand her any more than she understood him. Their lifestyles were at complete variance. Still, she continued to think of him, to watch him, to wonder. He was crowding her mind.

As she sat in his study, reading over a draft of a new

chapter, Kasey recognized that on this level, at least, they were reaching a firm compatibility. He was capturing the feelings she was trying to project to him, then intermingling them with dry facts and data. It was proof of her own usefulness. Being of use was essential to her.

Kasey laid the papers back in her lap and looked over at him. "It's wonderful, Jordan."

He stopped typing and, lifting a brow, met her eyes. "You sound surprised."

"Pleased," she corrected. "There's more empathy in this than I expected."

"Really?" The statement seemed to interest him as he leaned back in his chair and studied her.

It made Kasey uncomfortable. She felt that he was intuitive enough to see through her if he chose to. That, she wouldn't care for. She rose and walked to the window.

"I think you might delve deeper into the two subcultures of Plains life. The semi-agricultural tribes of the eastern plains lived in villages and had traits of the Plains as well as the eastern and southeastern cultural areas. They consisted of—"

"Kasey."

"Yes, what?" She stuck her hands in her pockets and turned back to him.

"Are you nervous?"

"Of course not. Why should I be?" She began to search for her pack of cigarettes.

"When you're nervous, you go to the window or"—he paused and picked up her cigarettes—"go for these."

"I go to the window to see what's outside," she countered, irritated with his perception. She held out her hand for her cigarettes, but he put them down on the desk and rose.

"When you're nervous," he went on as he crossed to her, "you have a difficult time keeping still. Something has to move—your hands, your shoulders."

"That's fascinating, I'm sure, Jordan." She kept her hands firmly in her pockets. "Did you take a course in psychology from Dr. Rhodes? I believe we were discussing the sub-cultures of the Plains Indians."

"No." He reached over and twined one of her curls around his finger. "I was asking you why you were nervous."

"I'm not nervous." She struggled to keep her body perfectly still. "I'm never nervous." A smile moved over his face. "What are you grinning at?"

"It's very rewarding to unnerve you, Kasey."

"Look, Jordan—"

"I don't believe I've seen you angry before," he commented, then took his other hand to her throat. Her pulse was beginning to hammer. Desire stirred inside him as it played under his palm.

"You wouldn't like it if you did."

"I'm not at all sure," he murmured. He wanted her. Standing there, he could all but feel the movement of her body under his. He wanted to touch her, to explore the sharp angles of her body and the softness of her skin. He wanted her to give herself to him with the enthusiasm that was so much a part of her. If he had ever wanted a woman as much before, he couldn't remember. "It's always interesting to watch a strong person lose control," he told her, still caressing her throat. "You're a very strong woman, and very soft. It's an arousing combination."

"I'm not here to arouse you, Jordan." Her body yearned for him. "I'm here to work with you."

"You do both very well. Tell me . . ." His voice slid over her skin as gently as his fingers. "Do you think of me when you're alone at night, in your room?"

"No."

He smiled again. Though he drew her no closer, Kasey felt the needs battering inside her. She was unaccustomed to restraining passion, unused to feeling it necessary.

"You don't lie well."

"Your arrogance is showing again, Jordan."

"I think of you." His fingers roamed to the back of her neck and tightened. "Too much."

"I don't want you to." Her voice was weak, and that frightened her. "No, I don't want you to." Shaking her head, she pulled away from him. "It wouldn't work."

"Why?"

"Because . . ." She fumbled and became more frightened. No one had been able to do this to her before. "Because we're looking for different things. I need more than you'd be able to give me." She ran a hand through her hair and knew she had to escape. "I'm going to take a break. We can pick up after lunch."

Jordan watched her dash from the room.

She's right, of course, he thought, frowning at the closed door. Everything she says makes perfect sense. *Why can't I stop thinking about her?* He walked around his desk and sat back down at the typewriter. She shouldn't appeal to me. Leaning back, he tried to dissect what he felt for her and why. Was it simply a physical attraction? If it was, why was he suddenly drawn toward a woman who was nothing like any other woman he had desired? And why did he find himself thinking of her at odd moments—when he was shaving, when he was in the middle of structuring a paragraph? It would be best if he simply accepted his feelings as desire and left it at that. There wasn't room for anything else. She was right, he decided. It wouldn't work.

He turned back to his notes, typed two sentences and swore.

✑✑✑

DASHING THROUGH THE PARLOR ON HER WAY TO HER room, Kasey spotted Alison sitting primly on the sofa, reading. The girl looked up, and her eyes lit.

"Hi." Kasey could feel nerves and longings still running through her. "Playing hooky?"

"It's Saturday," Alison told her. She gave Kasey a hesitant smile.

"Oh." She would have had to be blind not to see the needs in the child's eyes. Setting aside her own problems, she sat next to Alison. "What're you reading?"

"*Wuthering Heights.*"

"Heavy stuff," Kasey commented, flipping a few pages and losing Alison's place. "I was reading Superman comic books at your age." She smiled and ran a hand down Alison's hair. "Still do, sometimes."

The child was staring at her with a mixture of awe and longing. Kasey bent down to kiss the top of her head. "Alison." She swept her eyes down the girl's blue linen pantsuit. "Are you attached to that outfit?"

Alison looked down and stammered. "I—I don't know."

"Do you have any grubbies?"

"Grubbies?" Alison repeated, experimentally rolling the word around on her tongue.

"You know, old jeans, something with a hole in it, a chocolate stain."

"No. I don't think—"

"Never mind." Kasey grinned at her and set the book aside. "With all the clothes you have, one outfit shouldn't be missed. Come on." Rising, she took Alison's hand and pulled her to the patio door.

"Where are we going?"

Kasey glanced down at Alison. "We're going to borrow the gardener's hose and make mud sculptures. I want to see if you can get dirty." They stepped outside.

"Mud sculptures?" Alison repeated as they wound their way around to the garden.

"Think about it as an art project," Kasey suggested. "An educational experiment."

"I don't know if Haverson will let you have a hose," Alison warned.

"Oh, yeah?" Kasey grinned in anticipation as they approached the gardener. "We'll see."

"Good day, miss." Haverson tipped the brim of his cap and paused in his pruning.

"Hello, Mr. Haverson." Kasey gave him a flash of a smile. "I wanted to tell you how much I admire your garden. Particularly the azaleas. This." She touched a funnel-shaped blossom. "Tell me, do you use oak leaves as mulch?"

Fifteen minutes later Kasey had her hose and was busily manufacturing mud behind a clump of rhododendron bushes.

"How did you know all of that?" Alison asked her.

"All of what?"

"How did you know so much about the flowers? You're an anthropologist."

"Do you think a plumber only knows about pipes and grouting sinks?" She smiled over at Alison, amused by the concentration on the child's face. "Education is marvelous, Alison. There's nothing you can't know if you want to." She turned off the hose and crouched down. "What would you like to make?"

Gingerly Alison sat beside her and poked at the mud with a fingertip. "I don't know how."

Kasey laughed. "It's not acid, love." She plunged in, wrist deep. "Who's to say Michelangelo didn't get his start this way? I think I'll do a bust of Jordan." She sighed, wishing he hadn't popped into her head. "He's got a fascinating face, don't you think?"

"I suppose so. But he's rather old." Alison, still cautious, began to work the mud into a pile.

"Oh." Kasey wrinkled her nose. "He's only a few years older than I am, and I'm barely out of adolescence."

"You're not old, Kasey." Alison looked up again. Her eyes were suddenly intense. "You're not old enough to be my mother, are you?"

Kasey fell in love. Her heart was lost, and there was no turning back. She was needed. "No, Alison, I'm not old enough to be your mother." Her voice was soft, understanding. When the girl dropped her eyes, Kasey lifted her chin with a fingertip. "But I'm old enough to be your friend. I could use one, too."

"Really?"

The child was crying out to be loved, to be touched. Kasey felt a wave of anger for Jordan as she cupped Alison's face in her hands. "Really." She watched the smile start slowly until it bloomed over the child's face.

"Will you show me how to make a dog?" Alison demanded and stuck her hands into mud.

When they walked back to the house an hour later, they were giggling. Each carried a pair of mud-caked shoes. Kasey's mind was clearer than it had been for days. *I need her as much* as she needs me, she thought and glanced down at Alison. She laughed and stopped to lift the child's streaked face.

"You're beautiful," Kasey told her. Bending, she kissed her nose. "However, your grandmother might disagree, so you'd better get upstairs and into a tub."

"She's at a committee meeting," Alison commented and giggled again, seeing the mud on Kasey's cheek. "She's always at meetings."

"Then we won't have to bother her, will we?" Kasey took Alison's hand and began to walk again. "Of course, you're not to lie to her. If your grandmother asks you if you were building mud sculptures behind the rhododendrons, you have to confess."

Alison pushed her untidy hair behind her ear. "But she'd never ask me anything like that."

"That simplifies things, doesn't it?" She pushed open the patio door. "I liked the dog you made. I believe you have artistic talent." As they walked through the brocaded parlor, Kasey began to search her pockets for a match. The room jangled her nerves.

"I liked your bust better. It looked just like—*Uncle Jordan!*"

"Yes, it was rather good." Kasey stopped at the foot of the stairs and dug in her back pockets. "You know, I never seem to have a match when I need one. I wonder why that is." Then, noting Alison's stunned expression, she glanced up. "Oh, hello, Jordan." She smiled amiably. "Have you got a light?"

He came down the steps slowly, looking from girl to woman. Alison's linen pantsuit was splattered with dirt. Her hair had escaped from its band and had traces of mud clinging to it. Her eyes stared out at him from a thoroughly dirty face. Her hands were brown past the wrists. So were Kasey's. A dozen reasonable explanations coursed in and out of his mind and were discarded. If he had learned nothing else during the past days with Kasey, it was to explore the unreasonable first.

"What the hell have you been doing?"

"We've been engaged in art appreciation," she returned easily. "Very educational." Kasey gave Alison's hand a squeeze. "You'd better go see about that bath, love."

Alison's eyes flew from her uncle's to Kasey's. She scurried up the stairs and disappeared.

"Art appreciation?" Jordan repeated, staring after his niece. He frowned back at Kasey. "You look as if you've been wallowing in mud."

"Not wallowing, Jordan. Creating." She pushed her own untidy hair out of her eyes. "We've been building mud sculptures. Alison's very good."

"Mud sculptures? You were playing in mud? We don't even have any mud."

"We made some. It's really very easy. You just take some water—"

"For God's sake, Kasey, I know the formula for mud."

"Of course you do, Jordan." Her voice was soothing and calm, but he caught the laughter in her eyes. "You're an intelligent man."

He could feel his patience ebbing. "Would you stay on the point?"

"What point was that?" She gave him a guileless smile that nearly turned into a grin as he heaved a deep breath.

"Mud, Kasey. The point was mud."

"Well, there's little else I can tell you about that. You said you knew how it was made."

He swore as his fingers tightened. "Kasey, don't you think it's a bit juvenile for a grown woman to take an eleven-year-old girl and spend the afternoon in a mud pile?"

So you know how old she is, Kasey thought and gave him a long look. "Well, Jordan, that depends."

"On what?"

"On whether you want an eleven-year-old girl for a niece or a forty-year-old midget."

"What the hell are you talking about? Even for you, that's hard to follow."

"The child is bordering on middle age, and you're so wrapped up in Jordan Taylor, you don't see it. She reads *Wuthering Heights* and plays Brahms. She's neat and quiet and doesn't intrude on your life."

"Just a minute. Back up a bit."

"Back up a bit!" Her anger had a habit of springing quickly. She pushed at her hair again. "She's just a little girl. She needs you, needs someone. When's the last time you talked to her?"

"Don't be ridiculous. I talk to her every day."

"You *speak* to her," Kasey countered furiously. "There's a wealth of difference."

"Are you trying to tell me I'm neglecting her?"

"I'm not *trying* to tell you anything. I *am* telling you. If you didn't want to hear it, you shouldn't have asked."

"She's never complained."

"Oh, *damn*!" She whirled away, then spun back again. "How can such an intelligent man make such a ridiculous statement? Are you really so insensitive?"

"Be careful, Kasey," he warned.

"If you don't like being told you're a fool, you shouldn't behave as one." She was past caring how angry he became. Her own temper—her own sense of justice—ruled her words. "Do you think that being housed, fed, and groomed are enough? Alison's not a pet, and even a pet merits affection. She's starving right in front of your eyes. Now, if you'll excuse me, I'd like to wash this mud off."

Jordan took her arm before she could walk by him. Turning her around, he propelled her into a powder room down the hall. Without speaking, she turned on the water and began to scrub. Jordan said nothing as her words played back in his mind. In silence, Kasey cursed herself steadily.

She hadn't meant to lose her temper. Though she had planned to speak to him about Alison, she had intended to broach the subject diplomatically, calmly. The last thing she had wanted to do was pour out her thoughts in a torrent of abuse. It had always been her opinion that the more you shouted, the less you were heard. She continually told herself not to become emotional when dealing with Jordan Taylor. She continued to do so. Now she took the towel he held out to her and carefully dried her hands.

"Jordan, I apologize."

His eyes were steady. "For what, precisely?"

"Precisely, for shouting at you."

He nodded slowly. "For the delivery but not the content," he commented, and Kasey sighed. He was not an easy man.

"Exactly. I have a tendency to be tactless."

He noted the way she was running the towel through her hands. She was ill at ease, he observed, but she wasn't going to back down. He felt a stir of reluctant admiration. "Why don't you start again?" he suggested. "Without the shouting."

"All right." Kasey took a moment to organize her approach. "Alison came to introduce herself to me the night I arrived. I saw an impeccably groomed young girl with shiny hair and beautiful manners. And bored eyes." Her sympathies were freshly aroused at the memory. "I can't accept boredom, Jordan, not in a child with her whole life ahead of her. It broke my heart."

Passion was back in her voice, but it was passion of a different kind. It wasn't anger this time. She was pleading with him to see as she saw. Jordan doubted she was even aware of the intensity of her eyes. She was thinking of the child only. Her compassion moved him. It was one more surprise.

"Go on," he told her when Kasey paused. "Say it all."

"It's none of my business." Kasey pulled the towel through her hands again. "You're perfectly free to tell me so, but it won't make any difference in how I feel. I know what it's like to lose parents—the rejection, the terrible confusion. You need someone to help you make sense of it, to fill the holes you don't even understand. There's nothing as devastating as the death of people you love and depend on." She took a deep breath. She was telling him more than she had intended to but couldn't seem to stop. "It isn't something you get over in a day or a week."

"I'm aware of that, Kasey. He was my brother."

Her eyes searched his and found something unexpected. He had loved deeply, too. All of her guards dropped away. She reached out to touch his hand. "She needs you. Jordan, there's nothing like the love of a child. They don't put conditions on their emotions. They simply give. There's a purity to it we lose when we grow up. Alison's waiting to love someone again."

He looked down at the hand that lay on his. Thoughtfully, he turned it over and studied her palm. "Do you put conditions on your emotions?"

Kasey's gaze remained level. "Once I give them, no."

He studied her a moment with a small frown of concentration in his eyes. "You really care about Alison, don't you?"

"Yes, of course I do."

"Why?"

Kasey stared at him in honest confusion. "Why?" she repeated. "She's a child, a human being. How could I not care?"

"She's my brother's child," he returned quietly. "And it would seem I haven't cared nearly enough."

Touched, she lifted her hands to his shoulders. "No. Not understanding and not caring are totally different."

The simple gesture moved him. "Do you always forgive so easily?"

Something in his eyes had warnings hammering in her brain. He was coming too close to the core of her again. Once he was there, Kasey knew she'd never be free of him. "Don't canonize me, Jordan," she said glibly. It was her most successful defense. "I'd make a dreadful saint."

"You're not comfortable with compliments, are you?" She started to drop her hands, but he placed his on top of them to keep them on his shoulders.

"I love them," she countered. "Tell me I'm brilliant, and I turn to putty."

"Oh, compliments on your intelligence. You're used to them, I imagine." He smiled. "On the other hand, if I were to tell you that you were a very warm, very generous person whom I find difficult to resist, you'd reject that."

"Don't do this, Jordan." He was too close, and the door shut them off from the rest of the house. "I'm vulnerable."

"Yes." He gave her an odd look. "That, too, is a surprise."

He lowered his mouth to taste her. At the first touch, he felt her fingers tighten on his shoulders. Then she relaxed and gave. For the second time that day, Kasey fell in love.

She felt the loss of her heart as a physical sensation, painful this time. He'll hurt you, her mind warned, but it was already too late.

"You smell of soap," he murmured as his mouth roamed over her face. "And there are a dozen freckles on your nose. I want you more than I've ever wanted another woman." His voice grew husky. "Damn you, I can't understand it."

When his mouth came back to hers, Kasey could taste the flavor of anger. His tongue probed deep as he pulled her closer. For the first time in her life, Kasey gave all—body, heart, mind.

When his hands reached for her, she offered no resistance but let them roam. Reason, she knew, would return all too swiftly. She pulled him closer, wanting to fill herself with the taste of him. Her fingers combed through his hair, then wandered down to the muscles of his shoulders and back. She wanted his strength—a strength to match her own.

He slipped both hands under her shirt to cup her breasts. Her skin was impossibly soft—as soft and warm as the inside of her mouth. He heard her moan as his thumbs brushed over her nipples. It was madness, he knew, but he wanted nothing else but to have her. Desire was pushing him as it never had before. There was a temptation to pull her to the floor and take her, quickly, fiercely, and be done with it. Would sanity return then? Would his life become his own again?

He pulled her away abruptly and stared down at her. Her breathing was quick, and the vulnerability she had claimed was all too apparent in her eyes.

"I need you," he said tersely. "And I don't like it."

"No." She nodded, understanding the feeling all too well. "Neither do I."

"And if I come to your room tonight?"

"Don't." Kasey pushed her hair back from her face with both hands. She had to think, yet thinking was impossible when she could only feel. "We're not ready, either of us."

"I'm not sure we have a choice anymore."

"Maybe not." She took a deep breath and felt her balance begin to return. "But for a while, why don't we stay out of bathrooms together?"

He laughed and caught her face in his hand. He had never known anyone else who could so easily make him laugh. "Do you really think that's going to help?"

Kasey shook her head. "No, I'm afraid it isn't, but it's the best I can do at the moment."

CHAPTER FOUR

A LISON SAT ON THE PINK SATIN SPREAD AND watched Kasey apply her makeup. The pots and tubes of color that were scattered over the vanity table fascinated her. Approaching, she began to finger them hesitantly.

"When do you think I'll be old enough to wear makeup?" Alison picked up a pot of eye shadow for closer study.

"Not for a few years," Kasey murmured as she darkened her lashes. "But with that face of yours, you won't need illusions."

Alison leaned over to peer at both faces in the glass. "But you use it, and you're much prettier than I am. You have green eyes."

"So do cats," Kasey commented and grinned. "Brown

eyes are very effective, especially on a blonde. Nothing devastates the human male more than soulful brown eyes and long lashes. You'll have boys eating out of your hand when you're fifteen." She watched Alison smile and blush. "Just don't turn on the charm too early," she warned and gave Alison's hair a tug. "And no fluttering eyelashes tonight. I don't think Dr. Rhodes could handle it."

With a giggle, Alison sat down on the edge of the lounger. "Grandmother says Dr. Rhodes is a distinguished man and a social asset."

I'll bet she does, Kasey mused to herself and picked up her lipstick. "I thought of him more as a teddy bear, myself."

Alison covered her mouth and rolled her eyes. "Kasey, you say the strangest things."

"Do you think so?" She began to search for a misplaced brush. "I thought it an accurate description. He's all round and kind of cuddly. Winnie the Pooh with glasses. I've always been fond of Winnie the Pooh. He's rather sweet and helpless and wise all at once. Have you seen my brush?"

Alison picked it up from the lounge chair and handed it to her. "He pats me on the head," she said with a sigh.

Stifling a grin, Kasey tried to convince her hair to come to order. "He can't help it. Older men who are confirmed bachelors have a tendency to pat children on the head. They really don't know what else to do with them." Kasey picked up her perfume bottle and aimed a squirt at Alison. She liked hearing the child laugh. "Let's go see if Pooh's here yet."

They entered the parlor together. Spotting Harry Rhodes across the room, Kasey looked down at Alison and sent her a conspirator's wink.

Standing beside Harry, Jordan noted the exchange. He lost the thread of his friend's conversation. When was the last time he had seen Alison smile that way? When was the last time he had taken the time to look? He felt a quick pang of guilt. As a guardian, he realized, he couldn't be faulted. But as a surrogate father, he had failed completely. It was time to make it up to her—and to himself.

He laid a hand on Harry's arm to stop his dissertation, then crossed the room to his niece. "Well, I wasn't prepared for two beautiful females." He lifted Alison's chin with his hand and studied her. She was quite beautiful, he realized with a start. And more grown up than he had thought. "I'll have to lock you up before long if I want to keep you to myself."

Alison's eyes widened in surprise. The look alone had him berating himself for having taken her for granted. How could he have lived with her for so long and not have noticed? As he watched, Alison glanced up at Kasey in confusion.

Jordan felt a moment of panic as she looked at him again. Was it too late?

"Oh, Uncle Jordan." He saw Alison's heart leap into her eyes.

Love without restrictions. He felt something open inside him. "Oh, yes," he said quietly and touched Alison's cheek. "I believe I'll keep you."

"Alison," Beatrice called from across the room. "Where are your manners? Come say good evening to Dr. Rhodes."

Alison flashed a grin at Kasey and went to do her grandmother's bidding.

"Well, Jordan." Kasey swallowed hard and cleared her throat. "You're quite a man."

He looked back at her and smiled. "Tears, Kasey?"

"Don't." She shook her head and swallowed again. "I'll disgrace myself."

Briefly, his eyes swept to Alison. "I have you to thank for that."

"Oh, no. Please." Kasey shook her head more fiercely.

He took her hand and lifted it to his lips. "Yes. I have a feeling it's going to be a difficult debt to pay. I had love staring me in the face and didn't see it."

She studied him and let out a deep breath. You still do, she thought. It's just a bit more complicated. "Jordan, unless you want to send Dr. Rhodes and your mother into fits and soil that perfectly beautiful handkerchief you have tucked in your pocket, you'll change the subject and fix me a drink."

"All right." He kissed her fingers again. "For now."

⤙⊙⤚

THROUGH COURSES OF ONION SOUP, RACK OF LAMB, AND chef's salad, Harry Rhodes prompted Kasey with questions about the science of anthropology. He was unable, even with this second meeting, to equate the Kathleen Wyatt whose work he had read and admired with the quick-witted woman who sat across from him. She bounced from one subject to the next, occasionally making statements that left him completely baffled. Because he knew Jordan well, he was easily able to see that his friend's interest in her was not strictly academic. And because Kasey had come into the Taylor household on his recommendation, he worried. Had he, in fact, saddled Jordan with a problem rather than a solution?

Her knowledge in her field, however, was all-encompassing. By the time the peach flambé was served, Harry began to relax.

"Anthropology is not psychology," Kasey answered to one of his comments. "As a psychologist, Dr. Rhodes, you attempt to hold culture constant and explore mind and psyche. As an anthropologist, I attempt to hold mind and psyche constant and explore culture. I have a good book on the subject. Perhaps you'd like to borrow it."

"Yes." Her conversation seemed lucid and relieved his mind. "I'd very much appreciate that, Miss Wyatt."

"Fine. If I can dig it up, you can take it with you tonight." She took another scoop of dessert.

"I'm afraid all this is far above my head," Beatrice put in. She sent Harry a warm smile. She ignored Kasey completely. "You psychologists and anthropologists fascinate me with your theories and philosophies on life."

"Now, Beatrice, I'd hardly consider my theories fascinating," Harry put in modestly.

"I wonder what Kasey's philosophy on life might be," Jordan mused. He sent her one of his engaging smiles. "I'm sure we'd all be fascinated."

Kasey licked the back of her spoon. "From this anthropologist's point of view, Jordan . . ." She paused to pick up her wineglass. "Life is like a moustache. It can be wonderful or terrible. But it always tickles."

Jordan laughed as Harry took a rather deep swallow of wine.

Thirty minutes later the two men were closed off in the

game room. Jordan racked the balls on the pool table and listened to Harry's uneasy comments on Kasey.

"Harry, there's no need to be concerned." He indicated for the doctor to break. "Kasey's giving me everything I need, and more. I'm finding the store of knowledge in that strange brain of hers incredible."

"That's precisely the point." Harry broke and frowned. "She is strange."

"Perhaps it's the rest of us who are strange," Jordan murmured. Since she had walked into his life, he was no longer certain. "In any case, she knows her field like most people know the alphabet." He moved into position for a shot. "I'd never be able to get the depth I want without her." He shot, made his ball, and moved into the next position. "What's more, she's the most intriguing woman I've ever met."

"You're not getting personally involved with her?"

"I'm doing my damnedest." Jordan frowned as the five ball missed the pocket.

"Jordan, a personal involvement with her could interfere with your work. I told you before when I read your outline, it's Pulitzer potential. You already have the reputation."

"It might be wiser to finish the book before we start thinking about Pulitzers. Your shot, Harry," Jordan reminded him.

Harry made two balls and missed a third. As he shot, he

thought over his next words carefully. "Jordan, I had noticed you'd been a bit restless lately. I was going to suggest a vacation when the book was finished."

Jordan grinned and leaned over the table. He positioned his cue. "Are you trying to protect me from Kasey, Harry?"

"I wouldn't put it that way—exactly," Harry blustered and leaned against his stick. "I realize Miss Wyatt is quite attractive, in a rather unusual fashion. She's also unsettling."

"Hmm. Unsettling," Jordan murmured. "She does take over. There's nothing I could do about it if I was sure I wanted to. The one thing I am sure of is that she's opened a few doors for me I hadn't known I had closed."

"You're not becoming emotionally . . ." Harry searched around for the proper phrase. "Entangled?"

"Am I in love with her?" Jordan frowned. He sank the nine ball and scratched. "I haven't the faintest idea. I know I want her."

"My dear boy," Harry began, "sex is . . ." He faltered and cleared his throat.

"Yes?" Jordan prompted, failing to suppress a grin.

"A necessary part of life," Harry finished stiffly.

"Harry, you surprise me." His grin widened. "Your shot." Both men glanced over as the door burst open.

"God, Jordan, you really should post road maps."

Kasey strolled in carrying a thick book. "I've never seen so many corridors. Your book, Dr. Rhodes." She set it on a table and blew her bangs from her eyes. "Have I trod on sacred ground?"

Jordan leaned on his stick. Why was it that a room seemed to come to life when she walked into it? "Would it matter?" he asked her and smiled.

"Of course not. I'm always treading on sacred ground. Can I have a drink?"

"Vermouth? I haven't stocked tequila down here."

"Yes, thanks." She was already involved with a survey of the room.

It was large and open with a gratifying absence of silks and brocades. The wood-planked floor she had imagined in the parlor was in evidence, and there were simple bamboo shades at the windows. It was scrupulously clean, but there were signs of living. A fat candle had been burnt down half-way in its pewter holder. A collection of record albums were stacked on a shelf, one or two of them at odd angles.

"I like this room," she said, and walked to a glass table that held a few pieces of primitive pottery. "Very much," she added as she turned to accept the glass of vermouth from Jordan. "Thank you."

He wasn't sure why her approval pleased him, but he

knew it did. She tilted her head as if trying to see him from a new angle.

"This is your room," she murmured. "Like the study."

"I suppose you could put it that way."

"Good." She sipped at her drink. "I'm beginning to like you, Jordan. I almost wish I didn't."

"We seem to have the same problem."

With a nod, she moved away. "Pool, huh? Don't let me interrupt you. I'll just finish my drink before I head back into the maze." She glanced around the room again. It was the only room in the house, other than the study, where she felt comfortable. "I'd like to talk to you about the book when you've finished it, Dr. Rhodes."

"Of course." Her smile, he thought, was indeed very appealing. "Perhaps you'd like to join us for a game, Miss Wyatt," he offered, surprising himself.

"That's very nice of you." She smiled again and watched with affection as he straightened his shoulders. "I'm sure you're betting, though, aren't you?"

"That's not necessary," Harry said.

"Oh, but I wouldn't want you to change the rules for me." Kasey sipped again and eyed a pool stick. "What are the stakes? Perhaps they're in my range."

"I'm sure we can accommodate you, Kasey." Jordan paused to light a cigar. "How about a dollar a ball?"

"A dollar a ball," she repeated, and approached the table. "Let's see, how many are there?" She frowned and counted. "Fifteen. I suppose I can handle that. How do you play?"

"Rotation might be simplest," Jordan commented and glanced at Harry.

"Fine." The older man began to chalk his cue.

"Rotation," Kasey repeated, then smiled as Harry handed her his cue. "What are the rules?"

"The object is to sink the balls into the pockets in chronological order," Jordan explained. She was wearing earrings tonight, he noticed. Small silver hoops that caught the light. Even across the table, her scent reached out to him. He brought himself back. "Or hit the next ball in order into another and sink that one, or as many as possible. Hit the cue ball, the white one, knocking it into the other balls from the lowest number to the highest. The object is to clear all the numbered balls from the table."

"I see." Kasey frowned down at the green baize and nodded. "It certainly sounds simple enough, doesn't it?"

"You'll catch on, Miss Wyatt," Harry told her gallantly. "Would you like to practice first?"

"No, why don't we dive right in?" She sent him another smile. "Who goes first?"

"Perhaps you'd care to break," Harry continued, feeling expansive as Jordan racked the balls again. "Just hit the cue ball into the rack. Whatever drops in is yours."

"Why, thank you, Dr. Rhodes." Kasey walked down to the end of the table.

"Hold the cue this way," Jordan instructed, positioning her fingers. "Keep it steady, but let it slide through. See?"

"Yes." She glanced over her shoulder at him. "I'm to smack it into the ball marked *one*, right?"

"That's one way to put it." He could kiss her now, he thought, right now, and send Harry into apoplexy. He could smell her hair as he stood over her, feel the smooth skin of her shoulder under his hand.

"I won't be able to hit anything on the table if you keep looking at me like that," she murmured. "And Dr. Rhodes is beginning to blush."

He stepped away. Kasey took a moment to steady herself, then bent over the table and shot.

She sank three balls on the break. Moving around the table, Kasey positioned and shot again. And again. She leaned over, narrowed her eyes to figure the angle and neatly sank the next ball. She stopped to chalk her cue while letting her eyes sweep the table to analyze the best strategy. The room was completely quiet.

She picked up her drink, took a quick sip and went back to work. There was a clatter and the thud of balls, then Harry's bluster as she executed a three-bank shot. Jordan watched her as she concentrated on the next quarry. Leaning on his stick, he enjoyed the view as she stretched out over the table in front of him and nipped the next ball into the pocket. She cleared the table, sending two balls into opposing corner pockets. Straightening, she rubbed her nose with the back of her hand and smiled at her opponents.

"Let's see, that's fifteen dollars each, isn't it? Would you like to break this time, Harry?"

Jordan threw back his head and laughed. "Harry," he said and patted the other man's shoulder. "We've just been hustled."

CHAPTER FIVE

J ORDAN STUDIED HER. KASEY WAS READING OVER A portion of his notes in silence. She had been quiet for more than twenty minutes. There was something inexplicable about the way she could switch the power off and on. She was teasing his mind as no other woman had ever done. When he asked her a direct question about herself, she answered, rambling agreeably but more often than not avoiding the real question. She revealed very little about Kasey Wyatt.

What secrets roamed around in that brain of hers? he wondered. What is it she's not telling me when she seems to be saying everything that comes to her mind? And why am I obsessed with learning it all? Jordan frowned at her and thought of the changes she had already brought into his life.

A child lived in the house now. There was laughter and noise and excitement. How long had he let things drift? For the three years Alison had been with him? And how long before that?

He had left the running of the household—and the responsibility of his niece—almost exclusively in his mother's hands. It had been simpler. Simpler, he reflected. His life, as a whole, had been simpler before Kasey had strolled through the front door. He had been content. And, he realized, like Alison, he had been bored. Harry had called it restlessness. There was little difference. No one in the household had been unaffected by her arrival.

His mother. Jordan frowned again and pulled out a cigar. Beatrice had already dropped a few subtle complaints. But then, he had learned to block out his mother's comments years before. For as long as he could remember, Beatrice had been involved in her committees, her designers, her luncheons. Both he and his brother had been turned over to a variety of nannies and tutors. Jordan had accepted it. Now, however, he wondered if he had been wise to put Alison's upbringing into her hands. Simpler, he thought again. But simple was often far from right. Apparently the time had come to take another look at things. He studied Kasey again. Quite a number of things.

"You're very perceptive, Jordan," Kasey commented, and pushed her glasses back up on her nose.

"Do you think so?" he asked. Once he would have agreed. Now he was beginning to wonder how much he had allowed to slip by him.

"You've explained your character's motivation very well here. It's beautifully done. I envy you."

"Envy me?" Jordan took a long drag. "Why?"

"Words, Jordan." She glanced up at him and smiled. "I envy you your words."

"I've noticed you have a supply of your own."

"Barrels of them," she agreed. "But I could never make them play like this." Jordan watched her eyes dart about the pages as she continued reading.

"You should understand, you get deeper into it in this section, the interaction between relatives in Indian culture," she pointed out.

"Families," Jordan murmured, thinking of his own.

"Yes. In many tribes, relatives administered public rebuke. Offenders were often exiled. That was tantamount to execution, as enemy tribes would more than likely kill an exiled Indian on sight."

"A father would send a son to his death?"

"Honor, Jordan. These were a people of honor and pride.

Don't forget that." She folded her legs under her and interlaced her fingers. "Murder was regarded as harmful to the entire tribe. Exile was the standard punishment. Not so different from what we do today. Behavior between relatives was often regulated by a strict code of rules."

"Kasey?"

"Yes?"

"May I ask you a personal question?"

She lifted her shoulders. She brought up her guard. "As long as I'm not required to answer it."

He studied the ash on the end of his cigar a moment. "Why did you become an anthropologist?"

She grinned. "Do you consider that a personal question? It's very simple, really. It was either that or the roller derby."

He sighed. She was going to take him on another detour. "God knows why, but I'm going to ask. What does the roller derby have to do with anthropology?"

"Did I say it did?" She took off her glasses and swung them idly by the frame. "I don't think so. I simply gave you my two career choices. I decided against the roller derby because it's a hazardous profession. All those bodies ramming into each other, and the floors are quite hard. I don't deal well with pain."

"And anthropology was a logical alternative."

"It was mine." She studied him a moment. "Did you

know the creases in your cheeks deepen when you smile? It's terribly attractive."

"I want you, Kasey."

The glasses stopped on the upswing. "Yes, Jordan, I know you do."

"And you want me."

She felt the thud of desire clearly, as if she were in his arms, his mouth on hers. "Perhaps I do." She dropped her eyes to his notes again and began to tidy them.

"Kasey." She brought her eyes back to his. "When?"

She knew what he was asking. She rose then, unable to sit. "It's not as simple as you make it sound, Jordan."

"Why?"

Turning, she stared out the window. *Because I'm in love with you,* she thought. Because you're going to hurt me. Because I'm terrified I won't be able to walk away when it's finished. Once I let you in, there'll be no turning back. "Jordan," she said quietly, "I told you I don't deal well with pain."

"Do you think I'll hurt you?"

She heard the surprise in his voice and laid her forehead against the glass. "Oh, God, I know you will."

When his hands came to her shoulders, he felt her muscles tense. "Kasey." He brushed his lips over the top of her head. "I have no intention of hurting you."

The ache was already growing, already spreading. "Intent, Jordan?" Her voice was thickening; he could hear the tears. "No, I don't think there'd be intent, but that wouldn't stop it." His fingers moved up to caress her neck. She could feel her control slipping away. "Jordan, please, don't." She started to pull away, but he turned her to face him.

He studied her carefully, brows lowered. Lifting his thumb, he brushed a tear from her lashes. "Why are you crying?"

"Jordan, please." Kasey shook her head. She knew she was losing. "I can't bear to make a fool of myself." Her own emotions were too strong for her, pressuring her. And his eyes were too direct and too demanding. She could feel the ground slipping out from under her. Longing, needs, fears were crashing down on her. The moment was fast approaching when she would have no choice but to give her emotions to him— without restrictions. "Let me go," she told him, struggling to compose herself. "I've given you enough this morning."

"No." His grip tightened. "Not enough. Not until you explain to me why you're falling apart in front of my eyes."

"Explain to you!" She threw back her head in sudden anger. "I don't have to explain anything to you. Why should I?"

"I think," he said slowly, "a more valid question is: Why shouldn't you?"

She was hurting, and her temper rose to protect her. "How

could I have said you were perceptive? How could I have thought that, when you don't see what's staring you in the face? I'm in love with you!" Her breath caught on a gasp of shock and dismay. They stared at each other, both rocked by the words.

"I didn't mean to say that." Kasey shook her head and tried to push away. "I lost my temper. I didn't mean to say that. Let me go, Jordan."

"No." He shook her once to stop her struggles. His eyes, as they stared into hers, were dark and intense. "Do you think you can tell me that, then walk out of here? No, you didn't mean to say it," he said slowly. "But did you mean it?"

There were no tears now. Her desperation had dried them. "If I said no?"

"I wouldn't believe you."

"Then it's academic, isn't it?" She tried to draw away again, but he held her still.

"Don't pull that on me now. It won't work."

"Jordan." Kasey's voice was steady again. "What do you want from me?"

"I'm not sure." He loosened his grip, abruptly aware that he must be hurting her. "Are you in love with me, Kasey?" She started to back away, but he shook his head. "No. Look at me and tell me."

She took a long breath. "I love you, Jordan. There're no

strings attached. I know some people are uncomfortable being loved. I don't understand it."

"As simple as that?" he murmured.

"As simple as that," she agreed and smiled. The weight of holding back was gone. "Don't frown, Jordan," she told him. "Being loved is easy. It's the loving that's difficult."

"Kasey." He hesitated. She had moved him, unsettled him, until he was no longer certain what he was feeling. "I don't know what to say to you."

"Then it's best not to say anything." This isn't easy on either of us, she thought and tried to smooth the path a bit. "Jordan, I'd like to explain myself to you. I'd do it better if you weren't touching me." After a moment he released her and she stepped back. The absence of contact helped steady her nerves. "I told you I loved you. That might have been a mistake, but it's done. I'd like you to accept it as it's given."

Kasey could see he didn't understand. Emotions, given freely, were always difficult to understand. How could she explain to him something that her heart had accepted over the objection of her mind?

"All of my life," she continued, "I've been taught that to give love, to express love, isn't so much a choice but an obligation. Please, just take it and don't ask me any more questions now."

"I don't even know what questions to ask." He wanted to touch her again, to hold her, but the expression in her eyes stopped him. He didn't want to hurt her, didn't want her to be right about that, too. "Kasey, don't you want anything from me?"

"No." She answered him quickly, as though she had anticipated the question. "I told you there were no strings, Jordan. I meant it. I don't think we can work together any more today, and I certainly don't think we can talk rationally about this right now. It's late, in any case. I told Alison I'd let her beat me at tennis before dinner." She was already heading for the door.

"Kasey."

It cost her a great deal to turn back around. "Yes?"

His mind had gone from crowded to blank. He felt like a fool. "Thank you."

"You're welcome, Jordan."

She managed to get through the door before the pain started.

❧

IT WAS COMPLETELY DARK BEFORE KASEY FOUND A moment to be alone. From the window in her room, she could watch the moon rise. It was full, with an orange tint that had her thinking of fields being harvested and haystacks. What is happening in the world out there? she wondered. I've been in this house too long, trapped by a love that's going to lead me nowhere. What have I done to myself? It's taken me a month to lose something I've valued more than anything else in all of my life: my freedom.

Kasey wrapped her arms around herself and turned back into the room. Even when I walk away from here, from him, I won't be free again. Love binds you—I knew that.

And what's he feeling now? What will we say to each other tomorrow? Can I continue to be casual, to hand out wisecracks as though nothing's changed? She laughed a little and shook her head. I have to, she reminded herself. Always finish what you start—isn't that Kasey's first rule? I came to do a job, and the job has to be done. I gave him my love without strings, and I have to follow through. Oh, God, she thought and hugged herself tighter. How I hate to hurt. What a coward I am.

Pressing a hand against her temple, she walked into the bath to search out her aspirin. It'll help the headache, she decided, if nothing else. As she reached for a cup, she heard a sound from Alison's room. Frowning, Kasey paused to listen.

It was quiet and muffled, but the sound of weeping was unmistakable. Kasey set down the aspirin bottle and went next door. Alison was bundled under the blankets, sobbing into her pillow. Everything but the child fled from Kasey's mind.

"Alison." She sat on the edge of the bed and touched the tangled blond hair. "What's wrong?"

"I had a nightmare." She threw her arms around Kasey's neck and clung. "It was horrible. There were spiders everywhere." She burrowed deeper as Kasey's arms came around her. "Crawling all over the bed."

"Spiders." Kasey squeezed and stroked. "Terrible. Nobody should have to handle them alone. Why didn't you call me?"

Alison could hear the steady beat of Kasey's heart under her ear and felt the comfort. "Grandmother says it's rude to disturb someone when they're sleeping."

Kasey controlled a swift, powerful wave of fury and kept her hands gentle. "Not if you have a nightmare. I used to yell like crazy when I had them."

"Did you really?" Alison lifted her face. "Have nightmares, I mean."

"The worst. Pop used to say it was the price of a creative imagination. He made me almost proud of them." She brushed the hair away from Alison's cheeks. "One more thing," she added. "You could never disturb me, Alison."

With a sigh, Alison laid her head back on Kasey's breast. "They were big spiders. Black ones."

"They're gone now. You should try kangaroos. Thinking about kangaroos is much better than thinking about spiders."

"Kangaroos?" She could hear the sleepy smile in the child's voice.

"Absolutely. Snuggle down." When Alison obeyed, Kasey slipped into bed beside her.

"Are you going to stay with me?" Her voice was small and amazed.

"For a little while." She drew the child against her and felt warm. "About those kangaroos."

"Kasey."

"Hmm?" She looked down to find Alison's solemn brown eyes on her.

"I love you."

Here it was, Kasey realized. Without condition, without demand. Pure love. Until that moment she hadn't known just how much she had needed it. "I love you, Alison. Close your eyes."

Jordan stood in the doorway and looked down on the two sleeping figures. Alison's head rested in the crook of Kasey's shoulder. He had lost track of the time as he stood there, captivated by the picture they made. Each was turned into the other as if they had found something they had been looking for.

They both belong to me, he thought, surprised by the warmth that flooded through him. They had both loved him, and he had been blind to it. Now that he knew, what was his next move? Love wasn't as simple as Kasey had told him it was. He thought about the way they had looked at him—Alison, stunned and hoping; Kasey, exposed and frightened. Walking over to the bed, he watched them sleep.

Bending over, he moved Alison gently. She stirred once and then was still, deep in a child's sleep. Carefully he lifted Kasey into his arms. She murmured something, wrapped her arms around his neck and settled into his shoulder. There was something in the trust of the gesture that aroused him more than a planned seduction. He turned to carry her through the connecting doors. Kasey's eyes opened slowly to stare at him.

"Jordan?" She was disoriented, and her voice was thick with sleep.

"Kasey." He kissed her brow. How could she go from innocent to striking by merely opening her eyes?

"What are you doing?"

"Trying to decide whether to take you to your room or mine." He paused at the doorway of her room. "Why were you in Alison's bed?"

"Spiders." Kasey remembered and tried to clear her head.

"I beg your pardon?"

"She had a nightmare." She sighed. Kasey had never been one to wake up on a bounce. "What were you doing in there?"

"I've started to look in on her at night. Something I should have been doing long ago."

With a smile, Kasey touched his cheek. "You're a nice man, Jordan. I wasn't certain." She yawned and rested against his shoulder again. "You can put me down anytime." With barely any effort at all, she could have been fast asleep again.

"Kasey." He noticed the pillow and blankets on the lounge chair. "Why don't you sleep in the bed?"

"Claustrophobia," she told him drowsily. "Between the canopy and those bed-curtains, I feel like I'm in a coffin. I'm going to be cremated."

"It's a simple matter to change your room." She snuggled against him and sent a shaft of desire through him.

"No, it doesn't matter. The lounge is fine, and the staff already think I'm eccentric."

"I can't imagine why." Jordan put her down on the lounge and sat beside her. "You always smell of violets," he murmured. His mouth sought hers and found it soft and warm and giving. He knew the exact moment when sleep cleared from her brain.

"Jordan." Kasey was wide awake and throbbing. "You

have me at a disadvantage." She put her hands to his chest and held them firm.

"Yes, I know. I wondered if I ever would." He took one of her hands and pressed his lips to the palm. "I intend to take advantage of it, Kasey." He trailed a finger over her shoulder, down her breast. He could feel the nipple strain against the thin material. "Tonight," he murmured. "Now."

"Jordan." The needs were churning, demanding satisfaction. "I told you before, there's a matter of choice."

"You also told me, only a few hours ago, that you loved me." He lowered his mouth to hers again. Good God, he wanted her. No woman had ever made him ache like this. The desire was in his blood, in his bones. She might have a choice, but she left him none.

"I told you I loved you." Kasey called out the last ounce of strength. "I didn't tell you I would make love with you. You've got to leave me something, Jordan."

She couldn't allow it to happen. She knew that once she shared herself with him, once she gave, she would tie herself to him completely. It wasn't a simple matter of wanting to be touched or feel pleasure, it was a matter of needing to belong.

Jordan studied her in silence, still holding her hand in his.

She was defenseless again, as she had been when sleeping with the child. He wouldn't hurt her; he swore to himself that he wouldn't hurt her. But he couldn't leave her. When he released her hand and rose to go to the door that adjoined Alison's room, Kasey let out a quiet sigh. But he closed it and turned back to her. She sprang up, prepared to send him away.

"Kasey." He crossed to her but kept his hands by his sides. "Let me love you tonight. I need you. It's the first time in my life I've needed someone else."

There was no sending him away. She might have resisted a seduction. She would have refused a demand. She was powerless against a need. Kasey drew him into her arms.

His mouth was instantly desperate, crushing down on hers until they were both reeling. He held her close—tightly, as though he feared she would spring away from him. But what she had offered she would never take back. He tugged the nightgown from her shoulders, anxious to feel her skin. He thought again how thin she was, how he had to take care lest he snap her in two. But his hands refused to be gentle.

Kasey felt no pain, only rocketing pleasure. She could sense the urgency bursting from him. She wanted him to need her. For now, it was enough. She pulled him toward the bed.

And he was on top of her. She wanted his weight; she was impatient with the clothes that separated them. Her mouth hungered. She poured herself into him through the kiss. It grew long, deep, totally involved until his hands stopped searching for her. It calmed them both.

Slowly, with care, he began to undress her. There was no longer a pressing drive for quick release. He wanted to savor her. He took his lips to her throat, and her sigh of pleasure rippled through him. Still seeking but no longer desperate, he moved to her breast. Kasey pushed at his robe until she could feel his skin under her hands. She found the strength she wanted.

She let him take her deeper, slowly, with not so much tenderness as thoroughness; neither of them looked for tenderness now. That was for later, perhaps, when the heat was less intense and the strength was sapped. He nibbled at her breast, experimenting with textures and flavors. She slipped the robe from his arms, and then he was as naked as she. He flicked his tongue over her nipple, then made a leisurely journey back to her neck. The flavor there was dark and heated, drawing him.

She let her hands roam where they pleased, testing muscles, exploring the outline of ribs, skimming over hard, narrow hips. She was lost in the feel of him. He was everything she had wanted, and his lips on her neck were sending her into a delirium of pleasure. Wanting his taste again, she murmured to him so that he brought his mouth back to hers.

A storm was building. She could feel it in the texture of the kiss. Her body was already answering, moving under him, agreeing, demanding. The breath moaned out of her lips and into his. He slid his hand over her breast, down to her hip. Her thighs were slim and strong. Her fingers gripped his shoulders, her body ached with passion. She opened for him, already shuddering.

She was hot and moist. He wanted to see her without control. His own was ebbing quickly. Too quickly. He didn't want to end it. He wanted to keep touching her, tasting her. He wanted to keep hearing her moan his name. It aroused him to near madness. His blood was pounding, but still he lingered, letting his lips brush over her hip, his tongue trace over her stomach. He could hear her breathing—quick and short. She moved under him with complete abandon. She was totally his. He needed to know it and didn't question the reason.

When he brought his mouth back to hers, he knew she had lost all restraint, all control. He felt a surge of power knowing that he and he alone held the key to her. Then she took him and drew him inside her. His thoughts shattered. He was hers.

⋘⊚⋙

KASEY CURLED UP AGAINST HIM AND DRIFTED IN THE afterglow of drugged contentment. She felt no regrets. She loved. She knew only that she had found the man she had waited for her whole life. She would have him for as long as she would be allowed. Tomorrows could be dealt with when they came. Tonight she had everything she wanted.

Jordan lay quiet in the darkness. His body was relaxed. He hadn't realized the tension he had subjected it to over the past weeks. But his mind . . .

It's never been like that before, he thought, a bit dazed by the knowledge. I can't say that to her. She'd never believe it. I'm not sure I do myself. She pulls at me; I shouldn't let her. He closed his eyes and tried to sweep his mind clear. But she was warm and soft against him, and her hand was on his heart. Sweet Lord, I've just had her, and I want her again. She's like a narcotic. He wanted to be angry, to resent what she was doing to him, but he couldn't fight his way past the simple need for her. He heard her sigh and felt her head move as she looked up at him.

"Jordan?"

"Yes?" Before he could prevent himself, his hand reached down to stroke her.

"I completely forgot about the canopy. Isn't that odd?"

Glancing down, he saw the shine of laughter in her eyes. All the doubts and strain slipped out of his mind as he smiled. There was no resisting her. "A cure for claustrophobia?"

"Definitely." She rolled on top of him. "But a scientist always tests her theory several times. Would you be willing to donate your body to the experiment?"

"Definitely." He pulled her mouth down to his.

CHAPTER SIX

"THE NOMADIC TRIBES OF THE HIGH PLAINS LIVED almost completely on the buffalo. They had no agriculture and did little fishing." Kasey yawned and sat back in her chair. "Sorry." She smiled over at Jordan. "I had a late night."

Her casualness this morning wasn't a pretense. She was at ease. She had told him she loved him, she had acted on that love and she had no regrets. The tension she had felt before had come from fighting her own instincts and concealing the truth. "I wonder, Jordan, if I could momentarily abandon my values and ring for some more coffee." She yawned again.

He studied her as she took a long, luxurious stretch. "You don't like servants, do you?"

"Of course I do." Kasey leaned her elbows on her folded

legs. "What I don't like is having them. About that coffee, Jordan. I'd make it myself, but Francois doesn't like anybody mucking about in his kitchen."

"Why don't you like having them?"

"Jordan, I can't philosophize properly on three hours' sleep." She sighed when he only continued to study her. "What color are Millicent's eyes?"

"What the hell does that have to do with anything?"

"Only to point out that people rarely notice the people who serve them. I waited tables in college, and—"

"You were a waitress?"

"Yes, does that surprise you?"

"It flabbergasts me." He grinned at her. "I can't picture you balancing trays and scribbling orders."

"I was a terrific waitress." She frowned and pushed her glasses up on her nose. "What was I trying to say?"

"When?"

"How is it you can be so clear-eyed and annoying this morning when you didn't have any more sleep than I did?"

He smiled at that as he rose and walked to her. "Because I've been sitting here listening to you spout information on the Arapaho and various Plains tribes and thinking that the thing I want most to do is make love to you again." He pulled her to her feet. "Right now."

She accepted the kiss with a murmur of agreement. If she had one disappointment, it was that she had been unable to wake beside him that morning. But there had been Alison to think of. Last night, she thought now as her mouth heated under his, had been much too short. And the night to come was too far away.

"I don't think we're going to get much work done this way," she murmured.

"We're not going to get any done." Jordan slipped the glasses from her face and put them behind him on the desk. "Come on."

"Where?"

"Upstairs." He was already pulling her to the door.

"Jordan." Kasey laughed and tugged on his hand. "It's eleven o'clock in the morning."

"Ten minutes of," he corrected, glancing at the clock as they passed through the parlor.

"Jordan, you're not serious about this."

"Tell me that in half an hour." He was propelling her up the stairs. "Alison's in school, my mother is at one of her famous committees, and I want you." He opened the door to his room. "In my bed."

She was inside and locked in his arms. There was no denying his hunger. She was already dizzy from it. His mouth was ravaging hers as if he had been starved for the taste.

"Jordan." Kasey managed to breathe when his lips sought her throat. "We're hardly alone here."

"I don't see anyone else," he murmured as his lips trailed up to her ear.

She moaned and tried to keep her balance. "There are servants all over the house this time of morning." He pulled her to him for a brief, hard kiss, then released her. Kasey felt the earth tilt.

In two strides, Jordan was beside the phone. He lifted the receiver and pressed a button without taking his eyes from her. "John, give the staff the day off. Yes, the entire staff. Right now. You're welcome." Jordan replaced the phone and smiled at her. "Fifteen people are about to be very grateful to me."

"Sixteen," Kasey corrected. "Thank you, Jordan."

He crossed back to her. "For what?"

"For understanding that I needed to be alone with you. Really alone. It's important to me."

He lifted a hand to her cheek. She was becoming important to him, he realized. Very important. "You will have to make your own coffee, now," he murmured.

"What coffee?" With a smile, Kasey began to unbutton his shirt. "Would you like to hear my opinion of coffee?"

"Not now." Jordan felt the need pushing at him as she moved to the second button.

"Well, I suppose I might bore you with it," she mused, loosening the third button.

"The one thing I don't think you could possibly do is bore me."

Kasey's fingers stopped, and her smile spread slowly. "Thank you, Jordan. That's a very nice thing to say."

Deliberately, he took his fingers to the top button of her own shirt. "But if I were to tell you that you were the most generous, the most genuine, person I've ever known, you'd change the subject."

The warmth filled her and clouded her brain. She didn't know how to answer, was terrified she would overreact and spoil the moment. Being in love, she discovered, made it more difficult to harness the emotions—and more necessary. "Yes, I imagine I would. I'd probably say something like, 'Where do you get your shirts? This material is really marvelous.'"

"Kasey." Her eyes came back to his. "You're beautiful."

She laughed at that, instantly more at ease. "No, I'm not."

"You have a dimple at the right corner of your mouth when you smile. When you're aroused, your eyes darken and cloud so that the gold in them vanishes."

She could feel her pulse start to hammer, her skin flush with heat. "Are you trying to unnerve me, Jordan?"

"Oh, yes." He slipped her shirt from her shoulders. Then he took his hands down her breasts to her waist. "Am I?"

She was trembling. It stunned her. He had barely touched her, and her body was throbbing for him. He had too much power over her, in every aspect—heart, body, and mind. She resisted it. She had given him her love but refused to surrender her strength. He had to want her every bit as much as she wanted him. Kasey loosened his last button.

"You unnerve me, Jordan," she whispered and ran her hands up, slowly, over his stomach, ribs and chest. She could feel his muscles go taut under her palms. As she drew off his shirt, she pressed her lips to his shoulder. "You make me ache." She trailed her fingertips back down his sides and took her lips to his throat. "You make me want." She unhooked his slacks and let her fingers guide them over his hips. As her lips traveled down his throat, she heard his low moan of pleasure. She pulled him to the floor.

Passion had tastes. His skin was hot and moist from it

where she kissed him. She could feel the thud of his heart under her tongue. It was like a dream. Her body was drugged, but her mind was active. She wanted to know all of him—what pleased, what aroused. She followed instinct, letting her hands roam; when she felt a response, she let them linger. His body was well-muscled and lean, and it excited her. His needs excited her. She could feel them pouring out of him. For this one moment of time he was as vulnerable as she.

She left a slow, lingering trail of kisses as she journeyed back to his throat. His breathing roared in her ears. Tangling his fingers in her hair, he groaned her name and pulled her mouth to his. Passion exploded in the kiss. She felt it whipping at her—an incredible mixture of pain and delight. His teeth dug into her lip, and she moaned. This was no dream, but shattering reality. His hands were suddenly rough and bruising as he pushed her on her back. He entered her swiftly, violently, and plunged over the edge of reason. She went with him, clinging, helpless, strong. She knew she had stopped breathing. They were fused together by damp skin and desire. They rose and crested, again and again, until there were only drained bodies and empty minds.

He lay on top of her, his face buried in her hair, unable to move, though he knew she was too slight for his weight.

Her body was still trembling lightly under his. Jordan lifted his head. He wanted to see her in the full light of day, after his loving.

Her face was soft, her eyes still misted. He felt a pain, both unexpected and sharp, slam into his stomach. She smiled, and the pain grew. Could he want her again? So quickly? Surely that would explain the ache he felt by just looking at her. He lowered his mouth to hers, but it was tenderness that greeted him, not passion.

"Kasey." He kissed her cheek, not certain what he was about to say. The emotions he felt were utterly new to him. There was a bruise on her shoulder, and he lifted his head again to look at it. It was small and faint and fit the pattern of his finger. It horrified him. To his knowledge, he had never marked a woman before.

"What's wrong?" Kasey saw the shock in his eyes and followed their direction. She smiled a little when she noted the bruise. "You have strong hands," she commented.

His eyes came to hers. It was difficult for him; his feelings about bruising a woman were very defined. He found no excuse for it. Abruptly, he remembered the look on her face when she had told him he would hurt her. "Kasey." He shook his head. "I don't want to hurt you."

"Jordan." She recognized the deeper meaning in his

words and lifted her hand to his cheek. "I know you don't." When he rolled over on his back, she went with him to rest her head against his shoulder. "Don't think about tomorrow now," she murmured. "Let's take today. It's enough."

He pulled her closer, drawing her into the curve of his body. Today, he thought, and closed his eyes. "You're tired." He had heard the fatigue in her voice.

"You did say something about a bed," she returned, but she was content to stay where she was. Close to him.

He rose, and before her protest was complete, he lifted her into his arms. "You need to sleep awhile." When he laid her on the bed, Kasey reached out to him.

"Sleep with me."

Jordan pulled back the covers and drew her into his arms.

ᶜᵒᴼᵒᴼᵛ

IT WAS LATE AFTERNOON WHEN KASEY WOKE. SHE remembered when Jordan had left her, urging her to stay and sleep. She had pulled him back for a kiss that had led to another storm of loving. A glance at his clock told her he had left more than an hour before.

Lazy, she told herself and stretched. If he had still been with her, Kasey would have found it no effort to roll over and go back to sleep. She pictured him down in the study working. She still had a job, she reminded herself. She pulled herself from bed and dressed.

Halfway down the stairs, she heard Alison practicing the piano. Beethoven this time. A lovely piece played without interest. She paused in the doorway and watched. She's doing her duty, Kasey thought with a stir of sympathy.

"Did you know Beethoven was considered quite a revolutionary in his day?" Alison's head shot up at the sound of Kasey's voice. She'd been waiting to hear it since she'd returned from school. Kasey smiled and crossed to her. "His music is so full of power."

Alison glanced down at her fingers. "Not when I play it. Uncle Jordan said you were sleeping."

"I was." Kasey stroked a hand down Alison's hair. "You play very well, Alison, but you don't put yourself into it."

"It's important to have a firm basis in the classics," Alison stated. Kasey could hear Beatrice in the words and bit back a sigh.

"Music is one of the greatest pleasures in life."

Alison shrugged and frowned at the notes. "I don't think I like music. I might be tone-deaf."

This time Kasey struggled with a grin. "That could be a problem." An idea shot into her head. "Hang on a minute."

She bounded from the room. Alison heaved a sigh and

went back to Beethoven. She was still fighting with the notes when Kasey returned.

"This is a good friend of mine," Kasey informed her and set down a guitar case. "He's good company," she went on as she pulled the battered instrument from the case. "He travels well. I don't." She smiled at Alison and was satisfied that she had caught the child's interest. "I can take him with me on a dig or on a lecture tour, which makes him more practical for me than a piano. I need music." She began to tune the guitar as she spoke. Alison rose from the piano stool to take a closer look. "It relaxes me, pleases me, soothes my nerves. It's also nice to play and do the same for someone else."

"I never thought about it that way." Alison reached out to touch the neck of the guitar. "You can't play Beethoven on this."

"Oh, no?" Drawing on memory, Kasey began to play the movement Alison had been practicing.

Alison's eyes widened. She knelt down to watch more carefully. "It doesn't sound the same."

"Different instrument." Kasey stopped to cup the child's chin. "Different feeling. Music comes in all forms, Alison, but it's still music." Why doesn't anyone take the time to talk with this child? Kasey wondered. She soaks up words like a sponge.

"Will you play something else?" Alison settled down at Kasey's feet. "It sounds beautiful."

"Maybe you're not tone-deaf after all." Kasey smiled at her as she began to play again.

Jordan stood in the doorway and watched them. Would she ever stop surprising him? he thought. It wasn't her playing that surprised him. If he had learned she had conducted an orchestra, he wouldn't have batted an eye. He doubted there was anything she couldn't do. But her capacity to give and draw love overwhelmed him. Was she born with it? Did she learn it? Was she even aware of the power she had?

Alison loved her. He could see it in her eyes. She simply accepted Kasey for what she was and loved. There were no questions, no doubts. And Kasey gave it back to her in the same way. But I have doubts, he mused. And questions. She's right again. When we grow up, we lose the talent for loving without restrictions.

Kasey glanced up and saw him. A smile moved across her face. "Hello, Jordan. This is the music-appreciation hour."

He returned the smile. "Am I invited?"

"Uncle Jordan." Alison scrambled up and forgot to brush out the creases in her skirt. "You should hear Kasey play. She's wonderful."

"I did." He glanced at Kasey again. "You are."

"Alison was having a little difficulty with Beethoven," Kasey explained. "So I went upstairs for my friend. He's been helping me."

"He?" Jordan shot Alison a look as he sat on the sofa. He pulled her down on his lap. "Don't you think it's rather odd to call a guitar 'he'?"

Alison giggled and looked up at him. "I did, but I didn't like to say so."

"Very discreet." He nuzzled her neck.

Alison responded by flinging her arms around him and clinging. The depth of his reaction shook him. Kasey had told him there was nothing comparable to a child's love, but he hadn't fully understood. Now, with the small girl hugging him, he felt the total power of it. How had he missed it before? How had he ignored it? Closing his eyes, he held her close and let the sheer pleasure of unconditional love run through him. She smelled of powder and shampoo, and her hair was fine and soft against his cheek. His brother's child. His, now. And he'd already wasted too much time.

"I love you, Alison," he murmured.

He felt her grip tighten. "Really?" Her voice was muffled against his neck.

"Yes." He kissed her hair. "Really."

He heard her sigh and relax. She kept her face buried against his neck. He opened his eyes and met Kasey's.

She was weeping silently. When he looked at her, she shook her head violently as if to deny the tears. She rose, but he stopped her before she could dart from the room.

"Don't go" was all he said.

She turned back to look at him, then began to fumble for a cigarette. For the first time, he heard her swear at the lack of a match. She walked to the window and stared out.

I love them both, she thought, and rested her forehead against the glass. *Much too much. To see them together like this, to watch them find each other—the joy of it filled her.* She sighed and let the tears run their course. He had looked so stunned when Alison had put her arms around him. Kasey could see each emotion move through him.

How much time do I have before I lose them both? Taking a deep breath, she worked to bring herself under control. *I won't think about it now. I can't think about it now. When I opened the door, I knew it was going to shut in my face sooner or later.* She felt the pain ebbing. Kasey brushed the drying tears from her cheeks. She turned back just as Beatrice glided into the room.

"Jordan, I'll be leaving now. The Conway party." Seeing Alison on his lap, she frowned. "Is Alison ill?"

"No." He felt the child straighten and kept his arm around her. "Alison's fine. Enjoy yourself."

She lifted a brow. "You should be attending yourself. You shouldn't neglect your social duties."

"I'll have to neglect them awhile longer. Give my best to the Conways."

Beatrice sighed. As she turned to leave, she spotted Kasey's guitar. "What is this?"

"That's a guitar, Mrs. Taylor." Kasey stepped back into the center of the room.

"I'm aware of that, Miss Wyatt." Beatrice sent her an arched look. "What is it doing here?"

"It's Kasey's," Alison put in. She felt protected and secure in Jordan's arms. "She's going to teach me to play." She glanced up at Kasey, having taken this for granted.

"Is that so?" Beatrice's voice was clipped and frosty. "And what possible use would it be for you to learn such an instrument?"

"It's essential that a child develop an interest in music at an early age, don't you agree, Mrs. Taylor?" Kasey smiled and cut off the cold response Jordan had on the tip

111

of his tongue. He saw his mother's brow crease and he relaxed again.

"Naturally."

"I'm an advocate of introducing children to the classics, and all forms of music, in infancy. There have been some very interesting studies on the subject."

"I'm quite sure there have." Beatrice's eyes swept back to the guitar. "But—"

"The Spanish guitar, such as this one, was developed from Oriental models during the seventeenth century." Kasey had on her lecturing voice, and Jordan was struggling with a grin. His mother was definitely outmatched. "During the nineteenth and twentieth centuries a succession of Spanish virtuosos, including, as I'm sure you know, Andrés Segovia, have proven the guitar to be an important artistic instrument. I'm sure you'll agree that broadening Alison's musical abilities will be a tremendous asset to her when she takes her place in adult society."

Beatrice was still frowning but looked a trifle dazed. Kasey gave her a friendly smile. "That's a lovely dress, Mrs. Taylor," she added.

Beatrice glanced down at the mauve silk. "Thank you." She brushed absently at the skirt. "I had planned to wear my white voile, but it's rather cool tonight. One doesn't wear white when it's cool."

"Really?" Kasey's brows lifted curiously. "That dress doesn't appear very warm."

Beatrice sent her a disparaging glance. "I have a mink to wear over it." She turned and left the room, not at all certain how she had lost the upper hand.

"My, my, my," Kasey muttered. "Aren't I a fool?"

"A very cagey one," Jordan remarked. His mother had annoyed her, that was clear enough. But she had kept her temper much more under control than he would have. And there was still a trace of humor in her eyes. He laughed suddenly.

"Your grandmother has just been confused by a master," he told Alison. "Oriental guitars and seventeenth century." He shook his head. "Is there anything you don't carry around in that encyclopedia you have for a brain?"

Kasey was thoughtful for a moment. "No, I don't think so. Is there something you'd like to know?"

He tilted his head, amused at the challenge. "What's the capital of Arkansas?"

Alison giggled and whispered in his ear.

"Arkansas," Kasey murmured. Her gaze wandered to the ceiling. "Arkansas . . . south central United States. North boundary, Missouri; east boundary, Mississippi and Tennessee; south, Louisiana; west, Texas and Oklahoma. Twenty-fifth state as of June eighteen thirty-six. Arkansas has soil favorable to agriculture, numerous mineral deposits that include the only diamond mine in the United States and extensive forest areas. The name comes from a Siouan tribe, the Quapaw. There are no natural lakes of importance, and it has a relatively mild climate. Oh, yes." She held up a finger. "Little Rock is the capital as well as the largest city."

She dropped her eyes from the ceiling and smiled guilelessly at Jordan. "Would anyone like to take a walk before dinner?"

CHAPTER SEVEN

THE CLIMATE IN PALM SPRINGS WAS DRY AND WARM and sunny. The servants in the Taylor household were well-trained, solicitous. The food was invariably superb. And the monotony of it all was driving her crazy.

If Kasey could have loved Jordan less, she could have escaped. But as each day passed, she knew she was adding links to the chain that kept her there. The time she spent with Jordan on research was a stimulant, as was the time she shared with Alison. But there were long hours with only idleness, and she had never been able to cope with idleness.

In the night, in Jordan's arms, she could let herself forget everything else. But their hours together as man and woman were all too brief. When he would leave her bed, she was left with too much time to think. It was difficult for her to admit that for all her sophisticated education and free-thinking ideas, she was uncomfortable in an affair. Perhaps if the relationship could have been more open, she would have had less doubt. But there was a child to think of.

It was already December. For Kasey, time was running out. In another month, perhaps six weeks, her usefulness would be at an end. And what then? she asked herself as she stepped outside. How much longer could she put off thinking about the future? She should have been booking another lecture tour for January. She should have found out if the Patterson dig was going on schedule in March.

She stuck her hands in her pockets and stared at a palm tree. She needed to get away, she decided. She needed to start thinking about herself again. She had to write her doctorate. She shut her eyes against the glare of the sun.

If she didn't start to make the break soon, it would hurt much, much more when the time came. How would Jordan feel when she left? Kasey stepped from the patio onto the lawn. Would he feel as though he'd lost something? Or would he simply remember their time together as one pleasant autumn?

As someone who made it a habit to pick apart the human

brain, she found it strange that she couldn't fully understand Jordan's. Perhaps it was because he was more important than anyone else had ever been. Emotions clouded her intuition, and she couldn't see clearly. She was only certain of Alison.

She had the child's love. It was simple, open. At eleven, a child had no masks. How many does he have? she wondered, thinking of Jordan. How many do I have? Why do we insist on wearing them? She looked around again at the smooth, even lawn, the perfectly groomed trees and organized flowers. I have to get away from here, she thought again. I can't stand the spotlessness much longer.

"Kasey!"

She turned to watch Alison dart toward her a few steps ahead of Jordan.

And when I do go, she reflected, they'll have each other. That much I can take with me.

"We couldn't find you." Alison grabbed her hand and smiled up at her. "We wanted you to go swimming with us."

The simple request set off a chain of emotional reactions. They don't belong to you, she reminded herself as her heart reached out for them. You've got to stop pretending they do. She kept her eyes on the child, unwilling to deal with one of Jordan's intuitive looks.

"Not today, love. I was just going for a run."

"Swimming uses more muscles," Jordan commented. "And you don't sweat."

Kasey lifted her eyes to his. She watched Jordan's narrow immediately and recognized that he sensed something of her mood. She wasn't willing to be seen so clearly.

Smiling, she gave Alison's hand a quick squeeze. "I still think I'd rather run." She turned and streaked away.

"Something's wrong with Kasey." Alison looked up at her uncle, but he was watching Kasey dash for the wall that bordered the estate. "Her eyes looked sad."

Jordan glanced down at Alison. Her words had mirrored his thoughts. "Yes, they did."

"Have we made her sad, Uncle Jordan?"

The question struck him, and he looked up in time to see Kasey disappear through the side gate. *Have we?* Her capacity to feel was beyond anyone else's he had known. Didn't it follow that her capacity to hurt was just as great? Jordan shook his head. Perhaps he was reading something more into a simple mood.

"Everyone has moods, Alison," he murmured. "Even Kasey's entitled to them." When he glanced down at the child again, her eyes were still on the side gate. Jordan swung her up over his shoulder to hear her laugh.

"Don't throw me in!" She laughed and wiggled.

"Throw you in?" Jordan countered as if the thought had never occurred to him. He mounted the steps to the pool. "What makes you think I'd do a thing like that?"

"You did yesterday."

"Did I?" He glanced over his shoulder at the hedges and wall. Kasey was on the other side. It gave him an uncomfortable feeling. With an effort, he brought his attention back to Alison. "I hate to repeat myself," he said and tossed her in.

An hour later he found Kasey in the drawing room. The run hadn't helped her mood. He watched as she paced from window to window. He felt her restlessness.

"Thinking of making a break for it?"

Kasey whirled around at his voice. "I didn't hear you come in." She searched for an ease she couldn't find, then turned away again. "I've changed my mind," she told him. "This place isn't a museum, it's a mausoleum."

Jordan lifted a brow, then took a seat on the sofa. "Why don't you tell me what's wrong, Kasey?"

When she turned back, there was a flare of anger in her eyes. It was easier to feel anger than despair. "How can you stand it?" she threw out at him. "Doesn't the everlasting sunshine ever get to you?"

He studied her a moment, then leaned back against the cushions. "Are you telling me you're upset about the weather?"

"It isn't weather," she corrected. "Weather changes." Kasey pushed her hair away from her face with both hands. She felt a dull, throbbing ache at the base of her neck.

"Kasey." Jordan's voice was quiet and reasonable. "Sit down and talk to me."

She shook her head. She had no desire to be reasonable just yet. "It amazes me," she continued, "absolutely amazes me, that you can write the way you do when you've cut yourself off from everything."

His brow went up again. "Do you think that's an accurate statement? I live in a favorable climate, so I've cut myself off?"

"You're so damn smug." She spun back away as her hands balled inside her pockets. "You sit here in your sanitized little world without an idea as to how people struggle through life. You don't have to worry if your refrigerator breaks down."

"Kasey." Jordan struggled to keep his patience. "You're veering off again."

She turned back and stared at him. Why couldn't he understand? Why couldn't he see what was underneath it all? "Not everyone can rest on his laurels and bask in the sun."

"Oh, we're back to that." Jordan rose and crossed to her. "Why is it you consider my money a black mark on my character?"

"I have no idea how many black marks you have on your character," she retorted. "My objection to your money is that you use it to insulate yourself."

"From your viewpoint."

"All right." She nodded. "In my view, this entire section of California is an outrage: golf, furs, parties, Jacuzzis—"

"Excuse me." Alison stood in the doorway and stared at both of them. It was the first time she had seen either of them angry. Jordan stifled a reply and turned to her.

"Is it important, Alison?" His voice was calm, but his eyes weren't. "Kasey and I are having a discussion."

"We're having an argument," Kasey corrected. "People have arguments, and I never shout during a discussion."

"All right." He nodded at Kasey, then looked back at his niece. "We're having an argument. Would you mind giving us a few minutes to finish it?"

Alison took a step back but hesitated. "Are you going to yell at each other and everything?" There was more fascination than concern in the question, and Jordan held back a smile.

"Yes," Kasey told her. Alison took a long, last look, then darted for the stairs.

Jordan laughed before he turned back to Kasey. "She's apparently pleased at the prospect of a rip-roaring fight."

"She's not alone."

He studied Kasey a moment. "No, I can see she's not. Maybe you'd like to throw something. That's always a nice touch."

"Which do you want to lose?" she shot back, hating that he was controlled and she was not. "The Ming vase or the Fabergé box?"

"Kasey." He put his hands on her shoulders. Enough, he thought, was enough. "Why don't you sit down and tell me what this is really about?"

"Don't patronize me, Jordan." She stepped away from him, temper snapping. "I get enough of that from your mother."

There was little he could say to that, as he knew the truth of it. What he hadn't known was that Kasey had been touched by Beatrice's attitude in any way. Perhaps there were many things he still had to learn about Kasey. And perhaps the time to learn them was when she was upset enough to lower her guard.

"My mother has nothing to do with you and me, Kasey." His voice had softened, but he didn't reach out to her.

"Doesn't she?" Kasey shook her head. How could it be

that he didn't notice it or understand how difficult it was to make love with him in a house in which she had to deal with constant disapproval? "Well, that's one small point of disagreement. We have several others."

"Which are?"

"Doesn't it worry you that the most important thought in Alison's head in five years will be what dress she wears?"

"Good God, Kasey, what are you talking about?" Frustration made his voice as hot as anger made hers. "Will you come to the point of all this?"

"Point?" She shouted at him now, enraged by her inability to express her feelings and his inability to understand what she was trying to say. "What point is there when you've absolutely no concept of how I feel or what I need?" She shook her head again. "There is no point, Jordan. No point at all." With this, she fled through the patio doors.

Ten minutes later Kasey sat under an oak tree in the north corner of the lawn, trying to gain control of her emotions. She detested losing her temper. Nothing she had said to Jordan had made sense—to him and, barely, to herself. Honesty forced her to admit that it was basic fear that prevented her from speaking what was in her heart. She loved him too much for her own peace of mind.

Heart or intellect—which should she listen to? Her intellect told her she shouldn't love him. He didn't love her. Wanted her, needed her, perhaps, cared for her. All mild, pale words compared to love. Intellect reminded her that there were too many essential differences between them to make anything but the most transitory relationship possible. Intellect stated it was time to remember her priorities—her doctorate, her work in the field. It was time to pull up stakes and get back to it.

But her heart thrust the love on her. She was caught between the two—heart and intellect—and she was unable, for perhaps the first time in her life, to make a clear decision.

She pulled up her legs and rested her brow on her knees. When she heard Jordan sit down beside her, Kasey didn't move. She needed another moment, and he, sensing it, said nothing. They sat together, close but not close enough to touch, while a bird began to sing in the leaves directly above their heads. She sighed.

"I'm sorry, Jordan."

"For the delivery but not the content?" he returned, remembering the other time she had apologized.

She gave a quick laugh but kept her head on her knees. "I'm not really sure."

"I don't think I'd mind being shouted at if I knew why."

"Blame it on the waning of the moon," she murmured, but he slipped a hand under her chin and lifted it.

"Kasey, talk to me." She opened her mouth, but he cut her off before she could speak. "Really talk to me," he added quietly. "Without the clever evasions. If I don't know you, or what you need, it might be because you do your best to keep me from finding out."

Her eyes were very clear and directly on his. "I'm afraid to let you in any more than I already have."

Her candor unbalanced him. After a moment he leaned back against the trunk of the tree and drew her to his side. Perhaps the easiest place to begin to learn of her was through her background. "Tell me about your grandfather," Jordan requested. "Alison said he was a doctor."

"My grandfather?" Kasey stayed in the circle of his arm and tried to relax. The subject seemed safe enough. "He lives in West Virginia. In the mountains." She looked out at the even, cropped lawn. There wasn't a rock in sight. "He's been practicing for nearly fifty years. Every spring he plants a vegetable garden, and in the fall he chops his own wood. In the winter the house smells of wood smoke." She closed her eyes and, leaning against Jordan, let herself remember. "In the summer there are geraniums in the window box outside the kitchen."

"What about your parents?" He felt the tension seeping out of her as the bird continued to sing out overhead.

"I was eight when they were killed." Kasey sighed again. Each time she thought of them, the needlessness of their deaths swept over her. "They were taking a weekend together. I was with my grandfather. They were coming back for me when another car crossed a divider and hit them head-on. The other driver had been drinking. He walked away with a broken arm. They didn't walk away at all." Her grief had dulled with time but remained grief nonetheless. "I've always been glad they had those two days alone together first."

Jordan let the silence drift a moment. He began to see why she had understood Alison so quickly. "You lived with your grandfather afterward?"

"Yes, after the first year."

"What happened the first year?"

Kasey hesitated. She hadn't meant to go into all of this, but the lack of demand in his questions had eased the telling. With a shrug, she continued. "I had an aunt, my father's sister. She was a good deal older than he—ten, fifteen years, I think."

"You lived with her the first year?"

"I lived between her and my grandfather that year. There

was a dispute over custody. My aunt objected to a Wyatt living in the wilderness. That was how she termed my grandfather's home. She was from Georgetown, in D.C."

A memory stirred. "Was your father Robert Wyatt?"

"Yes."

Jordan was silent as he let bits and pieces fall into order. The Wyatts of Georgetown—an old, established family. Money and politics. Samuel Wyatt would have been her paternal grandfather. He'd made his fortune in banking, then had gone on to become a top presidential advisor. Robert Wyatt had been the youngest son. Two older brothers had found places in the Senate. The sister would be Alice Wyatt Longstream, congressional wife and political hostess. A very wealthy, very conservative family. As he remembered, there had been talk of grooming the youngest son for the top office in Washington.

He'd been a brilliant young lawyer. There had been a great deal of press when he was killed. And his wife . . . Jordan frowned as he tried to remember things he had read and heard seventeen years before. His wife had been an attorney as well. They had opened a law clinic together, something his family had not wholeheartedly approved of.

"I remember reading about the accident," Jordan murmured. "Then a bit now and again about the custody suit. My mother and father discussed it occasionally. She's acquainted with your aunt. There was a good deal of publicity."

"Of course." Kasey lifted a shoulder. "Wealthy political family squabbles with backwoods country doctor over child. What makes better press?"

Jordan heard the hint of bitterness slip into the careless words. "Tell me about it, Kasey."

"What's there to tell?" She would have risen then, but his arm kept her beside him. His hold was gentle but firm. "Custody suits are ugly, and hideous for the child caught in the middle."

"Both your parents were lawyers," Jordan put in. "Surely they had clearly defined wills giving you a legal guardian."

"Of course they did. My grandfather." Kasey shook her head. How was he able to pull so much out of her with only a few words? She never discussed this part of her life with anyone. "Wills can be contested, particularly if you have a great deal of money and a great deal of power. She wanted me, not for me, but because my name was Wyatt. I understood that even when I was eight years old. It wasn't difficult; she had never approved of my mother. My parents met while they were in law school. It was one of those instant attractions. They were married within two weeks. My aunt never forgave him for marrying an unknown law student who was only at Georgetown University because of a scholarship."

"You said you lived between your grandfather and aunt the first year. What did you mean?"

"Jordan, this was all very long ago—"

"Kasey." He interrupted her, turning her face to his. "Talk to me."

She settled back in his shoulder again and shut her eyes. The tension was back in her muscles. "When my aunt filed suit, things began to get ugly. There were reporters. They came to school, to my grandfather's house. My aunt hired a firm of detectives to prove he wasn't caring for me properly. In any case, I was having a difficult time dealing with it. My grandfather thought it might be easier for me if I lived with my aunt for a while. It would take some of the pressure off, and I might find that I wanted to live with her. At the time, I hated him for sending me away. I thought he didn't want me. I didn't stop to think that it was the hardest thing he'd ever done. I was all he had left of my mother."

Jordan watched her run her thumb over the gold band

she wore. "My aunt had a beautiful row house in George-town. Thirty-fifth Street. It had high ceilings and fireplaces in every room. Fabulous antiques and Sèvres china. She had a collection of porcelain dolls and a black butler she called Lawrence." Kasey started to rise again. She needed to move.

"No." Jordan kept her against him. "Sit." He knew that if she stood she'd find a way to avoid telling him any more. "What happened?"

"She bought me organdy dresses and Mary Janes and paraded me around. I was enrolled in a private school and given piano lessons. It was the most miserable time in my life. I hadn't gotten over my parents' deaths yet, and my aunt was far from maternal. She wanted a symbol—a nice, quiet child she could dress up and show to her friends. My uncle was away most of the time. He was nice enough, I suppose, but self-absorbed. Or perhaps that's not fair; he had a great deal of responsibility. Neither of them could give me what I needed, and I couldn't give them what they were looking for. I asked obnoxious questions."

He laughed a little and kissed her temple. "I'll bet you did."

"She wanted to mold me, and I refused to be molded. It's really that simple. I was surrounded by beautiful things I wasn't supposed to touch. Fascinating people came to the house whom

I wasn't supposed to speak to, except to answer, 'Yes, sir,' or, 'No, ma'am,' when I was addressed. It was like being caged."

"Your aunt dropped the suit."

"It took her three months to realize she couldn't live with me. She told me if there was any Wyatt in me it was well hidden, and sent me back to my grandfather. It was like being able to breathe again."

Jordan frowned out over the lawn. From where they sat, he could just see the top story of the house. Is she feeling caged here? He remembered the way she had walked from window to window in the drawing room. He wanted a little time to digest the things he had just learned about her. "You're very close to your grandfather," he murmured.

"He was my anchor when I was growing up. And my kite." She smiled and plucked at a blade of grass. "He's a caring, intelligent man who can argue three viewpoints at once and believe all of them. He knows me, accepts me for what I am and loves me anyway." She brought her knees up and again rested her forehead on them. "He's seventy, and I haven't been home in nearly a year. In three weeks it'll be Christmas. There'll be snow, and someone will give him a tree in lieu of payment. His patients will be flooding into the house all day, bringing him everything from home-baked bread to home-brewed whiskey."

She's thinking of leaving, he realized and felt a quick, unexpected panic. He watched the sun filter through the leaves and fall on her hair. Not yet, he thought. Not yet. "Kasey." He touched her hair. "I've no right to ask you to stay. Stay anyway."

She gave a rippling sigh. For how much longer? she wondered. I should go home until I recover from this, from him. Kasey lifted her head, prepared to say what she felt had to be said.

Jordan's eyes were on her. They were clear and seeking. He wouldn't ask her again; he wouldn't insist. Kasey realized he didn't have to. His silence—his eyes—were doing it for him.

"Hold me," she murmured and held her arms out to him.

There would be no leaving him, she thought as she pressed against him. Not until she no longer had a choice. She had opened herself to him, offered. She couldn't take herself back now.

Then he was kissing her softly, without demand. He'd not been this gentle before, holding her as if she were something fragile. No, there would be no leaving him now. Kasey's heart had more power over her life than her intellect. Where she loved, she was vulnerable, and where she was vulnerable, her mind had no sway. She pulled him closer.

The kiss grew deep, still tender, but intimate and weakening. His hand went to her cheek to stroke her skin. It was soft, so soft, and had needs hammering inside him. He murmured her name and traced his lips down to her throat. There was warmth there and a taste he had grown to crave.

How was it she could give him so much and ask for nothing? But there was something he could give her, give both of them. "Kasey, I have to go to New York this weekend. Some business with my publisher." He didn't add that he had been putting the trip off for weeks. "Come with me."

"New York?" Her brows came together. "You haven't said anything before."

"No. It depended on the progress of the book. Kasey." He kissed her again. He didn't want her to ask questions. "Come with me. I want some time with you, alone. I want more than a few hours at night. I want to sleep with you. I want to wake up with you."

She wanted it, too. To be with him, away from the house. To be able to spend the night with him in complete freedom. Kasey could feel some of the weight beginning to lift. "What about Alison?"

"As it happens, she asked me just this afternoon if she could spend the weekend with a school friend." Jordan smiled and brushed a curl from Kasey's cheek. "Let's consider it fate, Kasey, and take advantage of it."

"Fate." Her lips curved into a smile, and Jordan watched as it finally reached her eyes. "I'm a very strong believer in fate."

CHAPTER EIGHT

New York. The plane had landed in a miserable sleeting rain that was rapidly turning to snow. The streets were a sloshy, slippery mess, packed tight with cars. The sidewalks were crowded with people hurrying. Nothing could have delighted Kasey more. New Yorkers, she mused, were always hurrying. She loved them for it. And there wasn't a city she knew that appreciated the Christmas season more. Everywhere she looked there were decorations—trees, lights and glittering tinsel. And there were Santa Clauses everywhere.

She had tried to draw it all in on the cab ride from the airport to the hotel. Now, in the bedroom of the suite she would share with Jordan, she pressed her nose to the window glass and continued to look. There were lights and people and the muffled hum of traffic. It struck her how completely she had been starved for the sights and smells of humanity. She had needed the noise and the motion.

Jordan hadn't expected her to have this sort of enthusiasm for the city. From what she had told him of her childhood, he had thought she would prefer a rural setting. But she hadn't been able to see enough. She had been bubbling over in the taxi, pointing at this, laughing at that. Anyone would have taken her for a first-time visitor, but he knew she had spent several weeks in Manhattan in early fall.

"You act as though you'd never been here before," he commented.

She turned to smile at him. The glow was there again. He could almost forget the unhappiness he had seen in her eyes only a few days before. "It's a wonderful place, isn't it? So many people, so much life. And it's snowing. I don't know if I could have made it through December without seeing snow."

"Is that why you came?" He crossed to her to run a hand through her hair. "To see snow?"

"Naturally." She lifted her face to brush his mouth with hers. "I can't think of any other reason. Can you?"

"One or two occur to me," he murmured.

She slipped out of his arms to wander around the room. "Nice place," she commented and ran a finger over the dresser top. The faint smell of rich polish hung in the air. "Not my usual working conditions."

"We're not working."

She looked back at him over her shoulder. "No?"

"A party, a few meetings." He came to her again and turned her to face him fully. "I could have skipped the party and handled the meetings by phone if work had been the only purpose of our trip."

"Jordan, I know you did this for me." She covered his hands with hers. "I'm grateful."

"I did it for me, too." He drew her into his arms. What was she doing to him? He had known her two months, and she was rapidly becoming the most important thing in his life.

"Are we really alone?" she murmured. She felt the relief wash through her. "God, are we really alone?"

"Alone," he agreed and lured her mouth to his.

"How soon is that party?" She pushed the jacket from his shoulders and began to work on his shirt.

"An hour or so." His hands slipped up under her sweater.

"Tell me . . ." She nipped at his lip and felt his shudder of response. "Do you consider being late rude or fashionable?"

"Rude." He ran his fingers down to unbuckle the thin belt she wore. "Very rude."

"Let's be rude, Jordan." She opened his shirt and sighed when her hands slid around him. "Let's be terribly rude."

When they were naked on the bed, he took his time. They had time now for slow loving. Kasey slipped into a cloud of pleasure. Where he touched, she heated; where he kissed, she ached. He was careful to keep his hands gentle, remembering the bruises he had given her before. Her strength, her drive, made it difficult to remember her fragility.

Her skin was smooth and pale, with barely a trace of a tan line. Though she spent many of her free hours outdoors, she didn't tan easily. He could see the contrast of the bronzed color of his hand against the milky whiteness of her breast. He took his mouth to it and heard her moan. She was more responsive than any woman he had known. There were no inhibitions in her. She loved freely.

Very gently, he caught her nipple between his teeth and felt her arch beneath him as she catapulted from contentment into passion. He used his tongue to keep her trembling until she was breathless and spent. Her fingers dug into his shoulders. Her murmurs urged him to hurry. But he moved without rush to her other breast.

"Jordan." She could barely speak, for waves of need were pressing down on her. "I want you now."

"Too soon." He trailed his lips down her rib cage. "Much too soon."

His mouth roamed, and she continued to shudder. He slipped his fingers inside her, taking her to a violent peak.

Delirium. Kasey knew she had passed all reason. Pleasure could give no more, passion could take no more from her. Yet he continued to drive her. Every cell of her body was alive, humming. She was nearly panicked to have him and clutched at him, willing him to be as desperate as she. His hands seared over her and had her quivering.

Then his mouth was on hers again—hungry, urgent. He took it to her throat with his teeth digging into her skin. He had forgotten his vow to be gentle. He had forgotten everything but the feel of her thin, agile body beneath his—and his own desperation.

Need sparked need, and he was inside her. There was no longer time for slow loving.

⌘

JORDAN DECIDED HE DIDN'T GET USED TO KASEY AS time passed but only became more intrigued by her. The elegant co-op overlooking Central Park was crowded with members of the book world: writers, editors, literary agents and scions of publishing. But she was the vortex of it. Other women glittered in jewels: diamonds, sapphires, emeralds. She required none.

She sat on the arm of a chair, sipping champagne and laughing with Simon Germaine, the head of one of the top publishing houses in the country. J. R. Richards hung over her shoulder. He was on his fourth in a string of bestselling novels, each of which had made the transition to the screen successfully. Beside her was Agnes Greenfield, one of the toughest agents in the business. She had represented Jordan for ten years, and he decided this was the first time he had seen her grin. She'd smiled, sneered, and snarled, but never grinned. As he watched, Kasey laid a hand on Germaine's shoulder and said something that made him throw back his head and roar.

Kasey's eyes lifted and found Jordan's through the crowd. She smiled slowly as she brought up her glass for another sip. A shaft of desire shot straight through him, nearly setting him back on his heels. How does she do it? he demanded of himself. How can she make me want her when I'm still warm from having her? When am I going to get enough? He pushed the questions aside and wondered how long it would be before they could slip away and he could have her to himself again.

"The widening schism between elitist and popular literature has made it difficult for the average person to enjoy light, entertaining reading without feeling guilty."

Kasey lifted her brow at J.R. as Jordan approached. "I've read all of your books, and my conscience is clear." She sipped her champagne and smiled at Jordan.

It took J.R. a moment before he began to chuckle. "I think I've just been put in my place. I'm tempted to begin collaborating, Jordan, if I can find a partner like this."

"I've been trying to convince Kasey to write a book of her own." Germaine gulped down his straight scotch without a blink. He had a wide, florid face and a stone-gray moustache above his lip. Kasey thought he looked a bit like a children's TV show host she remembered from her own girlhood.

"I appreciate that, Simon." Kasey pushed her curls behind her ears and crossed her legs. "But I've always felt that being a writer meant being frugal with words. I'm very lavish with mine."

"You tell a hell of a story, Kasey." He patted her knee companionably, and she caught Jordan's lifted brow. "I've got editors to deal with the excess."

"And I'm temperamental." Kasey finished off her champagne and was immediately handed a fresh glass. "Thanks." She gave J.R. a friendly smile.

"What writer isn't?" Germaine huffed and pulled out a thick cigar. "Are you temperamental, Jordan?"

"Periodically."

"I'm difficult to work with all the time, which at least makes me predictable," Kasey put in.

"The one thing I've found you are not, is predictable." Jordan lifted his own champagne.

"The perfect compliment. Jordan, there's some fantastic-looking caviar over there. I wouldn't feel right if I didn't stuff myself."

They moved across the room to a sumptuously prepared buffet. He watched Kasey heap beluga caviar on a thin cracker. "You and Germaine seem to have hit it off nicely."

"He's sweet," Kasey said with her mouth full. She was already reaching for another cracker. "God, I'm starving. Do you realize what time it is, according to West Coast time? Did we eat on the plane? I can never remember anything that happens at thirty thousand feet."

"Sweet?" Jordan repeated, ignoring the rest. The adjective, applied to Germaine, was enough to arrest his attention. "I don't believe I've ever heard him described quite that way before."

"Oh, I've heard the stories." Kasey began to forage for something else and found a bowl of iced cocktail shrimp. "Heaven," she muttered, spearing one with a toothpick. "He's supposed to be tough as old leather and mean as a starved dog. What is this?" She pointed toward another platter.

"Beef tongue."

"We'll just skip over that," she decided. She helped herself to another shrimp. "I like him."

"Apparently, the feeling's mutual."

Kasey smiled and paused long enough to drink some champagne. "Your sensibilities were offended when he put his hand on my knee. You're terribly cute when you're reserved and conventional, Jordan. Would it embarrass you terribly if I kissed you right now?"

She was baiting him, and he knew it. Firmly, he put his hand behind her neck and pulled her close. Her eyes laughed at him before he gave her a long, hard kiss. She carried the strong, exotic flavors of the buffet. When he drew away, she was still smiling.

"Caviar's good, huh?"

"It seems I have a taste for it."

She turned and piled another cracker high. "Have some more," she invited with a grin. "I can't ever get enough of it myself."

He took a bite of the cracker she held up to his mouth. "I want you out of here," he told her quietly. "I want you alone, where I can take those clothes off you piece by piece."

"An interesting proposition," Kasey murmured, touching a finger to his tie. "Am I allowed to do the same to you?"

"Required."

"Jordan!" A woman glided up to them—sturdy, fortyish and unashamedly blond and busty. Kasey flipped through her memory file and drew out a newspaper picture of Serena Newport, highly successful novelist who wrote books stacked with swashbuckle and sex.

Serena kissed Jordan heartily on both cheeks. "You don't show up at these things often enough," she complained. "I like to be seen with classy men."

"Serena. It's good to see you."

"And who's this?" She gave Kasey a strong look. "Good God, thin as a rail and positively stunning. If I stand here for too long, I'll wind up looking like an albino elephant. Are you a writer, dear? And who colors your hair?"

"A fan, Miss Newport, and I was born with it."

"God, it's disgusting." She put her hand on an ample hip

and shook her head. "Not the fan part, dear, the hair. Born with it? Dreadfully unfair. And whose fan are you, Jordan's or mine?"

"Both." Kasey was liking her more with each passing minute.

Serena laughed in one short boom. "That's unusual. Not too many people read both *Last Abstinence* and *Passion's Victory*, do they, Jordan?"

"Kasey's unusual, Serena. Serena Newport, Kathleen Wyatt."

"And what do you do? I know." She held up a hand before Kasey could speak. "Don't tell me—you model."

"Model what?" Kasey asked, enjoying herself.

"Clothes. No—an actress," she stated, changing her mind. "That's a very expressive face."

"Thank you, but I don't act professionally. Only in day-to-day encounters."

"Quick, too," Serena murmured. "You're not an agent trying to lure Jordan away from Agnes?"

"Not if I value my life," Kasey replied.

"Well, my dear, I'm fascinated and totally baffled." Serena hailed a passing waiter and grabbed a glass of champagne. There were chunks of precious stones on her fingers, and her nails were a brilliant red. "What are you?"

"I'm an anthropologist."

"You're joking." Serena looked at Jordan for confirmation. "Is she joking?"

"You wouldn't ask if you questioned her on the tribal rituals of the Sioux," Jordan replied and finished off his drink.

"You don't say." Serena drew out the words.

"Kasey's collaborating with me on a book."

"Hmm." Serena took a healthy swallow of champagne. "You don't happen to know anything interesting about the Algonquins, do you, dear?"

"Originally a North American tribe who were dispersed by the Iroquois in the seventeenth century. Most found new settlements in Quebec and Ontario," Kasey countered.

"Fate!" Serena exclaimed and grabbed Kasey's arm. "Do you believe in fate, dear?"

Kasey shot a look at Jordan and grinned. "As a matter of fact, I do."

"I've just started a new book. The first half is in England, but the second half has my now-penniless aristocrat off to the colonies. He's half-starved and all but beaten to death when he comes upon a party of Algonquins. They wouldn't have scalped him or anything dreadful like that, would they?"

Kasey grinned. "Many of the Algonquins were friendly to white settlers for some time. It depends upon which tribe you are talking about. However—"

"Perfect. Wonderful." Serena folded Kasey's arm through her thick one. "I'm stealing her for an hour, Jordan. It's too good to miss. Have some more champagne." She gave his cheek a motherly pat. "I'll send her back to you when I'm done."

Kasey looked over her shoulder and shrugged as she was propelled away.

"IT'S THE FIRST TIME," KASEY SAID LATER, "THAT I'VE met anyone who can outtalk me." She leaned against the backseat of the cab, tucked into the curve of Jordan's arm. "I'm suitably humbled."

"I gave serious consideration to strangling her after the first hour." She was close, and the scent of her hair wafted over him. She was warm and a little sleepy, a little high on champagne. He wanted her. "She drilled you for two hours and ten minutes."

Kasey laughed softly. "She's a marvelous person."

"I've always thought so, until tonight."

"She's very fond of you." Kasey smiled up at him. "She

told me you were a wonderful writer, a marvelous man, particularly when you forget to be polite." She laughed at his lifted brow. "I had to agree with her."

"If Serena's books are a barometer, she prefers a more—earthy type."

"Oh, Jordan, I just love it when you're dignified." She took a nip at his ear. "Why don't you kiss me again the way you did at the party? Sort of macho and domineering."

"Damn you, Kasey." He was laughing as he pressed his lips to hers.

"*Mmm*, swear at me and I'm yours," she murmured.

"Be careful," he warned, finding his hunger growing despite her teasing. "I ran out of patience an hour ago."

Kasey laughed again and laid her spinning head on his shoulder. "And he burned for her, burned with a white-hot heat that only she could satisfy." She sighed and snuggled. "Serena Newport, *Chesterfield's Woman*."

She was more than high on champagne, Jordan realized. She was three-quarters drunk. "Kasey, you're smashed," he said, amused.

"Well put," she agreed. "You writers have a way with words." She lifted her mouth to just beneath his. "Are you going to take advantage of my condition?"

"Absolutely."

"Oh, good." She wrapped her arms around his neck. "Start now."

The cab pulled over to the curb, and Jordan untangled himself. "Why don't I pay off the cab first?"

"Details." Kasey stepped onto the sidewalk with the help of the doorman. The cold air, still smelling of snow, whipped over her cheeks. It did nothing to clear her head. "Jordan." She tucked her arm into his when he joined her. "It's just occurred to me, something you said in the cab about Serena's barometer. Does that mean you read her books?"

"Of course I read her books." He steered Kasey through the doors and across the lobby. "Does that surprise you?"

"I stand astonished."

"It's astonishing that you can stand at all," he countered, pressing the button for the elevator.

"But Jordan, I have a difficult time picturing you reading *Chesterfield's Woman*." Kasey allowed herself to be drawn inside the elevator.

"Why?" He pushed the button for their floor, then pulled Kasey into his arms. "To quote Germaine, she tells a hell of a story."

Then he was kissing her with a quick, desperate hunger that had her rocking on her feet. She would have been dizzy even without the help of champagne. The silk pressed cool against her skin as his hand ran down her back. The heat kindled in her slowly, until she was utterly pliant in his arms. Passion licked by wine simmered under his touch. Her mouth was soft under his, and his tongue moved inside to seek hers. Her thighs throbbed with need, and her head swam. She was reeling and heating and floating all at once. She could no longer cling to him but went limp in her first total surrender.

"God, Kasey, I've never known an elevator to take so long." He buried his face in her hair and tried to draw back his own sanity. She was so fluid, so totally willing to have him love her; he felt incredibly strong. He hadn't known he would find even her weakness an excitement when it had been her strength that had drawn him to her.

The elevator doors slid open, and he guided her out into the hall.

"Jordan." Kasey turned to him again, leaning against him with her face lifted to his. Her eyes were misted, but the smile reached them.

"What?"

"Do you remember what Chesterfield does to Melanie in chapter eight right before the ship is attacked by the British frigate?"

He grinned, remembering very well. "Yes, as it happens, I do. Why?"

"Well." She put her arms around his neck again. "I was wondering—a purely academic thought—if fiction could be translated to fact. I'm thinking of doing a paper on the subject."

"And you'd like me to help you test your theory?"

"Exactly." She ran her hand through his hair. "Would you mind?"

"In the interest of academia, I might be persuaded." He swept her into his arms. "Didn't it start something like this?" He slipped the key into the lock and carried her inside.

CHAPTER NINE

SHE WAS STILL ASLEEP WHEN HE WOKE. JORDAN immediately felt her warmth and the light tickle of her hair on his shoulder. The room was still dim, with the heavy curtains drawn over the windows, but a glance at his watch told him it was morning. He had a meeting scheduled in just over an hour. With a sigh, he looked down at Kasey.

He'd never known anyone who slept so deeply. He brushed the hair away from her forehead. She didn't even stir.

He thought of how she had been the night before—the sleepy sexuality, the husky laugh, the heavy eyes. If he had been a fanciful man, he would have thought her a witch. There was something otherworldly about her. Every time he thought he had power over her, he found himself caught in hers.

But now, as she slept, she might be any woman. Now she was just a woman sleeping off a night of champagne and loving. So how was it, he wondered, that she still pulled at him? As she slept, she couldn't dispense her cockeyed charm or send out those looks that both invited and challenged him. And yet he was drawn to her, even as she lay there. He lowered his mouth to hers.

Jordan kept his lips gentle, and Kasey didn't stir. He had wanted this—to wake beside her. To wake her. Her lips were so soft, he felt he could sink into them. He murmured her name and kissed her again. Her face was pale without makeup, and there was a light sprinkling of freckles over her nose. He kissed her cheek, and his hand sought her breast. She didn't wake, didn't stir, but sighed in sleep as though she dreamed of him. He found the pulse in her throat with his lips and felt it beat slowly. His own was already beginning to race.

He stroked gently, feeling his passion build. Knowing the thrill of possession, he ran his hand down the length of her. The skin on the inside of her thighs was water-soft. He moaned, shattered by his need for her.

He took his mouth to her ear, to her temple, then back to hers to part her lips urgently. Her response was slow as he pulled her from the dream, then her lips moved under his with a quiet moan. Her heart was suddenly pounding under his hand. He entered her before she was fully awake, spinning her into passion as delirious as his own.

She was curled against him again, her arms tight, her head resting in its favored spot in the curve of his shoulder. She sighed and kissed where her lips could reach easily. "Good morning," she murmured.

She brought out something primitive in him that he wasn't certain he was comfortable with. He'd never experienced the degree of passion she could draw from him. The laughter in her voice was irresistible. "Good morning. How do you feel?"

"*Mmm*, wonderful." She snuggled closer. "And you?"

"Fine, but *I* wasn't teetering on my feet last night." He shifted away just far enough to look at her. Her eyes were clear. The dimple at the corner of her mouth appeared as her lips curved. "No hangover? You're entitled to one."

"I never have hangovers." Kasey kissed him lightly. "I refuse to believe in them." She rolled over until she was leaning on his chest, looking down at him. "Do you realize how much trouble could be avoided if we simply didn't believe it?"

"An interesting theory."

"I have dozens of them."

"I've noticed." He smiled and ran a finger down her cheek. "Your theory last night was particularly interesting."

Kasey laughed and dropped her forehead onto his chest. "It worked."

"Beautifully."

"Shall we tell Serena?" She lifted her head again, and her eyes were bright with humor.

"I think not."

She kissed him again, lingering. "Do you remember I once told you that you had a terrific body?"

"Yes. I recall being surprised at the time. But I didn't know you as well then."

She sighed as she felt his hands lower to her hips. "I still think so." Kasey rested her cheek on his chest. There was a contentment in her she had never felt before. "You have meetings today, don't you?"

"Yes. I've one in . . ." He lifted his arm to glance at his watch. ". . . in about half an hour. I'm going to be late."

"If we were in Fiji," she murmured, "we could stay like this all day, and you wouldn't need that watch."

"If we were in Fiji," he countered, "you wouldn't have had your snow."

Kasey sighed again and closed her eyes. "You're so logical, Jordan. It's one of the things I love most about you."

He said nothing for a moment. She hadn't mentioned love to him since the first day she had confessed it. He had wanted to hear it again so that he could explore his own reaction. Now he could feel her beginning to drift back to sleep.

"I don't like to leave you alone," he murmured.

"There're a million people out there." She yawned and snuggled down. "I'll hardly be alone."

"I'd rather be with you."

"Don't worry about me, Jordan. I'm going to look for a sweatshirt and some jeans for Alison. Something cheap and symbolic that she can grub around in."

"For making mud sculptures?" He felt the smile tugging at his mouth again.

"Mmm-hmm." She smiled, remembering the expression on his face the first day she and Alison had made them. "And I want to see all the Christmas decorations. I'm going to have a lot more fun than you are."

"Can you break off from your busy schedule to meet me for lunch?"

"Hmm, maybe. Where?"

"Where would you like?" He knew he should be up and dressing, but he found it impossible to move.

"Rajah," she said drowsily. "West Forty-eighth Street."

"Two o'clock, then."

"Okay. Did I bring my watch?" she asked him.

"I've never seen you wear one."

"I keep it in my purse so it doesn't intimidate me."

He kissed the top of her head. "I have to get up. If I stay much longer, I'll have to make love with you again."

She lifted her face, and her eyes were half-closed. "Promise?"

He drew her back to him.

⌀⌀⌀

"TWENTY MINUTES LATE." AGNES GAVE HER WATCH A hard look. "That's not like you, Jordan."

"Sorry, Agnes." He settled back in a leather chair. Agnes sat behind a six-foot desk. It was piled with manuscripts and memos. Jordan had always felt that sitting behind that desk, she looked like a general waging battle.

"Well." She saw the humor in his eyes and leaned back, a pencil tapping on her lip. "I hope it was worth it."

Jordan lifted a brow and said nothing. Agnes had expected nothing else. She had never been able to bait him. A very cool character, she thought, not for the first time. She remembered the animated woman he had brought with him the night before. An interesting combination.

"About your collaborator," Agnes began, pushing a few papers aside. "Is she as good as you were led to believe?"

"Better," he told her.

She nodded. "Then it's money well-spent."

"I want her to have a percentage of the royalties."

"A percentage of the royalties?" Agnes scowled and shifted in her chair. "You contracted her for a flat fee."

"She's to have that as well." Jordan sat back and laced his fingers.

"Jordan, the fee you're paying her is very generous." Her voice was patient. "Your personal life is one thing, but business is business."

"This is business," he countered. Jordan's voice was patient, too, but firm. Agnes recognized the tone and stifled a sigh. As well as being cool and cautious, he was stubborn, and she knew it. "I never expected, when we wrote up the original agreement, that I'd be able to draw so much out of her. Agnes, the book's nearly as much hers as it is mine. She's entitled to benefit from it."

"Ethics." Agnes sighed. "You have such a sterling character, Jordan."

"So do you, Agnes." He smiled at her. "Or you wouldn't be my agent."

Agnes shrugged. "What percentage did you have in mind?"

⁂

KASEY FOUGHT HER WAY THROUGH GIMBELS AND LOVED every minute of it. She'd run into a sale and had three sweatshirts and two pairs of jeans tucked into her shopping bag. Shopping was something she did rarely, but when she did, she did it passionately. She could spend three hundred dollars on a dress without a qualm and haggle furiously over a five-dollar sweater. She pushed her way through the crowds and scrambled happily through racks of bargains as she shot from store to store.

Passing a window, she spied an inch-high pewter unicorn and rushed inside to dicker over the asking price. A pang of hunger reminded her of the time, and she began to search through her purse for her watch.

"Six twenty-seven," she muttered, frowning at it. "I don't think so." She tossed it back into her purse and smiled at the clerk who was boxing her unicorn. "Do you know what time it is?"

"One fifty." He responded to the smile.

Deciding she could make twenty blocks in ten minutes at an easy jog, she took off without hailing a cab. When she arrived at Rajah, her cheeks were flushed and her eyes were brilliant. She passed through the elaborate entranceway and stepped inside.

The heat rushed to meet her. It felt wonderful after the stinging cold, and she pulled off her gloves to stuff them into her bag.

"Madam."

She turned her smile on the maître d'. "Jordan Taylor."

"Mr. Taylor just arrived." He bowed in her direction. "This way, please."

Three hours of shopping and no breakfast had left her famished. Jordan watched her coming toward him and rose.

"Hi." She kissed him, then let him help her off with her coat.

"You were serious about the shopping, I see," he commented, glancing at the bag before she tucked it under the table.

"Deadly," she agreed as she accepted a chair. "I bought you a present. You can have it after I see the menu. I'm starving."

"Some wine first?" He gave the order to the captain at his elbow while Kasey buried her face behind the menu.

"The Crab Goa's always good. And the Barra Kabab." She put the menu down and grinned. "I think I'll have both. Shopping gives me an appetite."

"Everything seems to," Jordan commented wryly. He took her hand, needing to touch her. "I've watched you eat. It's amazing." He brought her hand to his lips. "Did you really buy me a present?"

"Yes. It's in the bag with Alison's sweatshirts." Kasey reached down to forage and brought up the box. "You can open it if you promise to order immediately afterward."

"Agreed." He lifted the top of the box and uncovered the unicorn.

"It's for luck," Kasey told him as the captain brought their wine. "You can't go wrong with a unicorn. I almost bought you a bumper sticker with a lewd saying, but I didn't think it would look quite right on your Mercedes."

"Kasey." Touched, he took her hand again. "You're outrageously sweet." Jordan tasted the wine and nodded to the captain. "The lady will have the Crab Goa and Barra Kabab. I'll have the Fish Curry."

"How hungry are you?" she asked when the captain withdrew.

"Hungry enough. Why?"

"I was wondering if I'd get any of your fish." She smiled when he laughed and slipped the small box into his pocket.

"So you bought me a unicorn and Alison sweatshirts. Did you buy anything for yourself?"

"No." She tossed her hair out of her eyes, then settled her elbows on the table and cradled her chin on her hands. "There were some earrings in the shop where I got the unicorn, flashy little drops in scrolled gold, but they wouldn't bargain with me. I was in the bargaining mood. And I got hungry." She grinned and reached for her wine. "How was your meeting?"

"Fine." He had debated discussing the royalties with her

and had decided against it. She might object, citing Agnes's argument about the original agreement, and in any case, he didn't want business to intrude on their time together. They had only one night left. "I've another one at four with Germaine. He'll probably ask me to use my influence to talk you into writing that book."

Kasey laughed and shook her head. "I think the writing's safer in your hands. But give him my best."

"What would you like to do tonight?" A basket of bread was placed before them, and Kasey dove into it immediately. "Would you like to see a play?"

"*Mmm*, a musical." She buttered the bread lavishly and offered him some. Jordan shook his head, smiling as she took a hefty bite. "Something with a lot of flash and a happy ending."

"I'll meet you back at the hotel at six?"

Kasey nodded, then reached for more bread. "Okay." Narrowing her eyes, she calculated the time between six and curtain. She smiled over the rim of her glass. "We'd better plan on having a late supper."

⌒⌒⌒

KASEY WAS DREAMING. IT WAS A FAMILIAR DREAM, TOO familiar, and her mind struggled to reject it before it took hold. She was alone, abruptly dropped down into a pure white sea in a small boat. She knew what would happen next and tried to push the image aside. But she wasn't strong enough.

The boat began to rock as the wind picked up, but she had no sail, no oars to guide herself. The water stretched as far as she could see. There would be no swimming for land. She was lost and alone and afraid. She was only a child.

When she saw the ship coming toward her, she shouted for it, steeped in relief. Her grandfather was at the helm, and raising a hand, he tossed out a lifeline. Before she could reach it, another ship floated up to her right. The wake of the two ships set her small boat rocking dangerously. Water hurled into her face and was soon ankle-deep on the deck. She was caught in the middle as each ship tried to draw her aboard.

She couldn't reach her grandfather's lifeline. The waves were knocking her around the boat until she screamed in frustration and begged him to come for her. He shook his head and drew the line away. She was sucked closer to the second ship. And the waves grew high until they tossed her into the sea. Water closed over her head, cutting off her air, her light.

"No!"

She shot straight up in bed, covering her face with her hands.

"Kasey." Her cry had roused Jordan from sleep. He

reached for her and found her cold and quivering. "What is it? What's wrong?"

"Just a dream." She fought for control. "I'm all right, it's nothing."

Her voice was shaking as desperately as her body, and though she resisted, he pulled her closer. "You're not all right. You're like ice. Hold on to me."

She wanted to do as he said but was afraid. Already she depended on him too much. She'd handled the dream alone before; she would handle it again. "No, I'm all right."

Her voice sharpened as she pulled out of his arms. She struggled out of bed and drew on her robe. When Jordan switched on the bedside lamp, she began to hunt for her cigarettes. He watched her as he reached for his own robe. There was no color in her face, and her eyes were dark with fright. She was shaking from head to foot, and her breath was still trembling.

Finding her cigarettes, she fumbled to pull one out. "I'm a scientist; I know what a dream is." She covered her mouth with her hand a moment, hearing the jerkiness of her own voice. Her teeth were chattering. "A sequence of sensations, images or thoughts passing through a sleeping person's mind. It's not real." She picked up Jordan's lighter, but her hand shook and she couldn't work it.

Quietly he crossed to her. Taking the cigarette and lighter from her hand, he set them back on the table. "Kasey." He put his hands on her shoulders, feeling her shudder convulsively under his palms. "Stop this. Let me help you."

"I'll be all right in a minute." She stiffened when he drew her close again. "Jordan, please. I can't stand to fall apart this way. I hate it."

"Do you have to handle everything by yourself?" He was stroking her back, trying to warm her. "Does needing comfort make you weak? If I needed to be held, would you turn away from me? Kasey, let me help you."

With a sob, she was clinging to him, her face pressed against his throat. "Oh, Jordan, it frightens me as much as it did the first time."

Without speaking, he picked her up and carried her back to bed. Keeping his arm tight around her, he drew her against his side. "You've had it before?"

"Since I was a child." Her voice was muffled against his chest. He could feel the racing of her heart. "I don't have it often anymore. Sometimes years." She closed her eyes and tried to steady her breathing. "When I have it, it's always the same, always so vivid."

Her trembling had lessened, but he kept her tight in the

circle of his arms. She was bringing out something new in him: the need to protect. "Tell me about it."

She shook her head. "It's just foolish."

"Tell me anyway."

She was quiet a moment, then, with a sigh, she began. Her description was short and her words were unemotional, but he could sense the feeling beneath them. It was childishly simple to understand, but then, it had been the dream of a child.

"I never told my grandfather about it," she went on. "I knew it would upset him. I only had the dream twice the whole time I was in college." Her voice had grown steadier and her hold on Jordan less desperate. "I had it once when I read a rehash of the custody case by some enterprising reporter who'd picked up on it when one of my uncles had been running for reelection. And again the night before graduation. I'd put that down to too much beer and the pressure of delivering the valedictorian address." She sighed now and felt her body relax.

"And since then?" He had felt the fear and tension pour out of her. Her body was warming..

"A couple of times. Once when Pop was in the hospital with pneumonia. It scared me to death; he's always bursting with health. Once on a dig. We'd had to shoot a rabid dog.

It broke my heart." She felt safe and grew sleepy again. Now she'd given him her trust as well as her love. She was content, for the moment, to be cared for. "That was two years ago. I don't know what set me off tonight."

He heard her voice thickening and said nothing. She'll sleep now, he thought and stared up at the ceiling. He wouldn't. His mind was too crowded with Kasey Wyatt.

When he had first met her, he had thought her a tough eccentric with a great deal of charisma. Now he realized there was far more to her than that.

Her breathing was even now, and quiet. Tomorrow they would return to Palm Springs to complete their work on the book. In another few weeks, Kasey would be finished with her work. Then it would be up to him.

Reaching beside him, Jordan found his cigars and matches. He lit one and smoked in silence while he listened to Kasey breathing deeply in sleep.

CHAPTER TEN

N LESS THAN TWO WEEKS IT WOULD BE CHRISTMAS. Kasey could feel the time rushing by her. The brief interlude in New York had done much to settle her. She felt in control again—of her nerves, of her situation. What she had with Jordan, she was able to accept again without all the doubts and discomfort that had been piling up. She loved him, needed to be with him. When the time came to pay the price, she'd pay it. Still, she wished time wouldn't move so fast.

For Alison's sake, she would have liked Christmas to come quickly, but for her own, she could wait. She would have drawn out each day, each hour. After Christmas would come the new year. With the new year would come the time for her to go.

Watching the child's simple pleasure helped to keep Kasey's mind off herself. For two short weeks she could spend her free time making the holiday come alive for the girl. The elegant red garland and silver bells that Kasey had seen the staff unpacking weren't really Christmas. She had spent one stiff, formal Christmas in her life. That was enough for her.

"Jordan!" Kasey dashed down the stairs and burst into Jordan's study. "You've got to see this. Come upstairs." She was pulling on his arm and laughing.

"Kasey, I'm in the middle of something here."

"Put it down," she ordered. "You work too hard." She leaned over and gave him a quick, hard kiss. "It's really terrific. You're going to love it," she promised. "Come on, Jordan, you can be back at work before your typewriter knows you're gone."

She was difficult to refuse under any circumstances, but when she was pulling on his arm and laughing like this, it was impossible. "All right." He rose and allowed her to drag him toward the stairs. "What is it?"

"A surprise, of course. I'm crazy about surprises." Upstairs she pushed open the door to her room and motioned for him to enter. He did, then studied the room in silence.

Red and green paper chains hung everywhere, crisscrossing and draping from wall to wall. They wound down the bedposts and framed the windows. Cardboard angels, Santas and elves hung from doorknobs and balanced on dresser tops, and a red felt stocking overflowed with candy canes. There was a bright gold star suspended from the center of the ceiling.

Jordan took a turn around and faced Kasey again. "Redecorating?"

"I didn't do it." She rose on her toes and kissed him again. He delighted her when he used that dry tone. "Alison did. Isn't it wonderful?"

"I can certainly say I'm surprised." Shaking his head, he looked around again. "And I can honestly say I've never seen anything quite like it."

"You should see the bathroom," Kasey told him. "It's spectacular!"

He smiled at Kasey and sent an elf spinning on its string. "And, of course, you told her you loved it."

"I do love it," Kasey countered. "It's one of the nicest things anyone's ever done for me. She wanted me to feel at home for Christmas. And now I do."

Jordan reached out to touch her hair. "If I had known paper chains would make you happy, I'd have made some myself."

Kasey grinned and threw her arms around him. "Do you know how?"

"I think I could manage it."

"Can you string popcorn?"

"Can I what?" He was distracted from kissing her hair.

"String popcorn," Kasey repeated, linking her hands around his neck. "What I'd really like to do on Christmas Eve is string popcorn for the tree. And I want to get Alison a puppy."

"Wait a minute." Jordan drew her away. "Sometimes it takes me just a minute to catch up."

"Just say yes to both and think of the trouble we'll save. I can't bear a tree without popcorn strings, Jordan. It's positively naked. And Alison needs a puppy."

"Why?"

"Why what?"

Jordan sighed and rubbed the bridge of his nose between his thumb and forefinger. How did she manage to do this so often? "Why does Alison need a puppy?"

"Because she wants one, first of all. That's a good reason." She smiled at him. "And a puppy would be a companion and a responsibility for her. What do you think about cocker spaniels?"

Jordan leaned back against the door. "I'm forced to admit I've never given them much thought."

"Give it a minute, then," she suggested. "It's a gentle breed, good with children. A pet is very important in childhood, Jordan. Owning one teaches a variety of valuable—"

"Wait." Jordan held up a hand to stop her. "It would be simpler if I just said yes and saved us both a lot of time."

"I told you that you were logical." Kasey smiled, pleased with herself.

Jordan put his hands on her shoulders. "I also think it's very thoughtful of you."

"So do I," she said lightly. "I'm a very thoughtful person."

"You are," he said and drew her closer. "Whether you like to hear it or not. You've made quite a difference in Alison's life—and in mine."

She couldn't speak but only laid her head on his chest. I love you both, she thought, and shut her eyes tight.

"Does this mean yes to the popcorn, too?" she asked him. It was so warm in his arms, so secure. It was impossible to believe that one day soon she'd have to leave them.

"I don't suppose I could face a naked Christmas tree."

She squeezed him. "Thank you."

"Now I've something to ask you."

She tilted her face back to his and smiled. "Your timing's exceptional," she decided. "I'm obliged to say yes to almost anything."

He kissed her nose. "Perhaps you'll remember that at a more opportune time, but for now you've probably noticed my mother doing quite a bit of sighing because I haven't attended any of the holiday parties."

"As a matter of fact, I have." Kasey kept her voice light. "I've also noticed," she said, "how expertly you ignore her."

"I've had a lifetime of practice," Jordan said dryly. "But there's a club dance at the end of the week. I should go. Come with me."

"Are you asking me for a date, Jordan?"

"It sounded like it." He laughed suddenly and shook his head. "Kasey, you make me feel as though I were sixteen. Will you come with me?"

"I like to dance." She slid her hands up behind his neck and linked them. "I'd like to dance with you." She gave him a kiss and let it slowly deepen until she heard his quiet sound of pleasure. "I believe I'll buy a new dress," she murmured. "Do you have a favorite color?"

"Green." His mouth roamed to her neck. "Like your eyes."

She laughed a little and pressed closer. "Jordan, there's one more thing I should tell you."

"*Hmm.* What?" His mouth was back on hers.

"Alison," Kasey began, accepting the kiss. "When she finished in here, she went to do your room."

"Do what?" he murmured, steeped in Kasey's taste.

"Your room."

"My room?" Jordan drew away a bit to look at her. "My room?" He glanced over her head at the paper chains and cardboard figures. Incredulity spread over his face as he looked back at Kasey. "*My* room?"

"Jordan, you're repeating yourself." Kasey laughed as he let out a long breath. Slipping her arms around his waist, she hugged him tightly. "You're going to love it," she promised. "You're getting a foam snowman."

∽⊙⑥∾

THE NEXT AFTERNOON, KASEY LOOKED ON AS ALISON strummed her guitar. The technique was still clumsy, but she made up for it with enthusiasm. Kasey thought back to the first time she had watched Alison sit stiffly at the piano, playing Brahms with precision and disinterest.

No more empty eyes, she thought and reached out to touch the girl's hair. What would it be like to have a child of her own? she wondered. She shook her head. She was becoming too sentimental and much, much too attached.

"Terrific," she told Alison when she had finished. "You learn quickly."

"Will I ever play as well as you?"

"Better, soon." Kasey smiled and packed the guitar in its case. "I've an affection for music. You've affection and skill."

"I didn't think so before." Alison sat down at the piano and began to finger the keys. "I can play things on the piano and the guitar now."

Kasey grinned. "Alison, I have to go shopping. Want to come with me?"

"Shopping?" Alison's attention was arrested. "Christmas shopping? I've finished mine, but I'd like to help you with what you have left."

"Have left? I haven't started yet."

"None at all?" Alison's eyes widened. "But there are only ten days left."

"That many?" Kasey rose and stretched. "Well, I suppose I can start early. I usually wait until Christmas Eve. I love the confusion."

"But what if you can't find what you want?"

How like Jordan she was, Kasey thought. "That's the challenge," Kasey told her. "I drive the salesclerks crazy." The thought made her grin. "In any case, I need a dress. We can grab a hamburger, too. There must be a McFarden's around somewhere."

"McFarden's?" Alison brought her brows together. She

was intrigued and cautious. So like Jordan, Kasey thought again. "I've never been to McFarden's."

"Never been to McFarden's?" Kasey gave her a look of exaggerated astonishment. "That," she said, "is positively un-American." Grabbing Alison's hand, she pulled her to her feet. "You need a lesson in patriotism."

Some time later, Kasey eased into a parking space. "I told you I'd find one." Switching off the ignition, she dropped the keys into her pocket. Alison climbed out, and Kasey locked up carefully.

"I hope Uncle Jordan won't mind that we borrowed his car."

"He told me I could use it whenever I liked." Kasey skirted around the Mercedes's hood.

"But Charles usually drives everyone except Uncle Jordan."

"Why should we drag poor Charles around?" Kasey countered. "We must have gone to a hundred and thirty-seven stores." She pushed through the glass doors. "I'm starving. Do you realize how long it's been since I had a hamburger?"

Alison looked around her and became caught up in the crowd and the noise. "It smells wonderful."

Kasey laughed and pulled her into line. "Smelling's not eating. I have a craving for French fries."

Alison stared up at the menu that hung above the counter and zeroed in on a picture of a hamburger. "I'd like one of those. Is it good?"

"Fantastic." Kasey laughed. "You have big eyes, Alison. Let's hope you have an appetite to match."

"It *is* big," Alison stated when they found a table. She took a bite and grinned. "And it's good."

"You have very discerning taste." Kasey dug into her own. She closed her eyes and sighed. "It's been too long. Do you think we can talk Francois into trying his hand at one of these?"

"You could," Alison stated and wolfed down a French fry.

"Why do you say that?"

"You could talk anybody into anything."

Kasey laughed and shook her head. "Perceptive little squirt, aren't you?"

Alison grinned and sampled her milk shake. "I've never seen anything like the present you got for Uncle Jordan."

"The shaman's rattle?" Kasey chewed thoughtfully on a French fry. "It was quite a find." It had been elegantly carved and painted. Apache. Kasey had been thrilled enough to come across it that she hadn't even thought to bargain. "It'll help him ward off evil spirits."

Alison was bulldozing her way through the hamburger.

———

"I liked the dress you bought, too. Green looks beautiful on you."

"I don't usually wear it. It's so obvious with my coloring." She sat back with her own milk shake. "Then, I don't mind being obvious now and again."

"It's very stylish," Alison told her and took another bite of her hamburger. "And slinky."

Kasey grinned. "I did like that other one, though. You know, the smashed velvet."

"Crushed velvet," Alison corrected and giggled.

"Whatever. Would you like an apple pie?"

Alison sat back and took a deep breath. "I don't think so. Would you?"

"Not if I want to get into that dress. What did you get me for Christmas?"

"It's a— Kasey!" Alison exclaimed.

"I thought I might catch you off guard."

"It's supposed to be a secret." Alison wiped her hands primly. "Telling would spoil it."

"Really?" Kasey gave her a guileless smile. "Is that why you've been creeping around the house and searching through closets?"

Alison blushed, then giggled again. "I only thought I might shake some boxes."

"That's an old story."

"Christmas is more fun with you here, Kasey." Her eyes were serious again. "Will you stay forever?"

Kasey felt the first crack in her heart. How could she explain to the girl what she didn't want to think of herself? "Forever is a long time, Alison." She kept her voice quiet and her eyes level. "I'll have to leave when my job's finished."

"But can't you stay and keep working for Uncle Jordan?"

"He doesn't need a resident anthropologist, Alison. And I've work of my own." She watched the child's gaze falter and drop. "Friends stay friends, Alison, no matter how far apart they are. I love you." She reached out to lay her hand over Alison's. "That's not going to change."

"Will you come back?" Alison lifted her eyes again. "And visit me?"

I can't, she wanted to say. How can you ask me? Can't you understand how it would hurt me? "You could visit me," she said instead. "Would you like that?"

"Really?" Alison's smile bloomed again. "And your grandfather?"

"Sure. Pop would love it." She began to pile things back on the tray. "You're much better behaved than I ever was. Why don't you dump all this stuff in the trash?"

Kasey took a moment when she was alone at the table to

pull herself together. It was better this way. Alison was already being prepared. And what about me? She shut her eyes a moment. I've said I'll pay the price when the time comes. I have to stick to that.

"Ready?" she said and gave Alison a smile when she came back to the table. "Now we have to find a post office so I can mail off those things to my grandfather. Do you think he'll like that little gnome with the buckteeth?"

When they entered the house, Alison was laughing, struggling to balance her share of Kasey's purchases. "I'll help you wrap them," she said, grabbing at a sliding box.

"We'd better get them upstairs first." Kasey rescued the box and glanced up as Beatrice came down the stairs.

"Alison, what have you been doing?" She frowned at the child's windblown hair.

"Alison helped me with my Christmas shopping, Mrs. Taylor."

Beatrice shifted her gaze and met Kasey's eyes. "I don't approve of you taking Alison from the house without discussing it with me first." She turned to her granddaughter again. "Go up and brush your hair, Alison. You look a sight."

"Yes, ma'am."

Kasey watched her walk obediently up the stairs. She turned back to Beatrice and spoke calmly. "I'm sorry if you were concerned, Mrs. Taylor. You were out when we left, and I did tell Millicent what our plans were."

Beatrice lifted a brow. "I dislike being informed by a servant of the whereabouts of my grandchild."

"It didn't occur to me you'd notice she wasn't here."

Beatrice's color flared. "Are you criticizing me, Miss Wyatt?"

"Of course not, Mrs. Taylor." Kasey fought to keep the conversation in perspective. "I enjoy Alison's company, she enjoys mine. We spent an afternoon together. I'm sorry if you were worried."

"I find your attitude impertinent."

"I can only repeat, I'm sorry," Kasey replied evenly. "Now, if you'll excuse me, I'd like to go put these things away."

"You'd be wise to remember your position in this house, Miss Wyatt." Kasey stopped, then set down her packages. It seemed they weren't through just yet. "You're a paid servant and can very easily be replaced."

"I'm here on a job, Mrs. Taylor, and no one's servant unless I choose to be." She paused a moment. "Is that all you have to say to me?"

"I won't tolerate your insubordination." Beatrice's knuckles whitened on the post of the banister. She wasn't accustomed to being looked at so directly by someone she considered an employee. "I won't tolerate your disruptive influence on my granddaughter."

"I was under the impression that Alison was Jordan's ward." What am I doing? Kasey thought abruptly. I'm putting Alison right between us. I'm putting her right in the middle. "Mrs. Taylor," she began, searching for a way to ease the tension for the child's sake.

"What's going on?" Jordan came through the drawing room doorway. He'd heard the argument the moment he'd stepped out of his study.

"This woman," his mother began, turning to him, "is insufferably rude."

Jordan lifted a brow. "Kasey?" he asked, turning to her.

"Probably," she agreed and tried to relax her muscles.

"Miss Wyatt took it upon herself to disappear with Alison for the entire afternoon, then had the effrontery to criticize me when I expressed concern."

Jordan, caught between amusement and annoyance, studied Kasey again. "Been busy, have you?"

"We only went Christmas shopping, Uncle Jordan." Alison came down half the stairs in a rush, then stopped when her grandmother turned to her.

"This is none of your concern, Alison. Go back up to your room."

"I don't think that's necessary." Jordan stepped around his mother and held out a hand to Alison. She dashed down the rest of the stairs. "Well, you appear relatively unharmed. Did you have a good time?"

"It was wonderful." Alison grinned up at him. "We went to McFarden's."

"Really?" Jordan shot a look at Kasey. He knew her well enough to see beyond the careless front. She was raging inside and, he thought curiously, hurting. What had been said, he wondered, before he had come upon them? He smiled at her, wanting to soothe her. "You might have asked me to go along."

Kasey was working to control her temper. She knew very well anger wasn't the way to handle Beatrice Taylor. And handling Beatrice Taylor would be necessary if she wanted to keep things smooth for Alison. It helped to see Alison standing under Jordan's arm.

"You were working," she returned. "And I didn't think the idea of tramping through shops would appeal to you."

"Kasey bought you a present, Uncle Jordan."

"Did she?" He drew the child to his side, but his eyes were on Kasey's.

"Chocolate cookies," Kasey told him. "Alison thought they were pretty."

"Obviously you intend to treat this matter lightly." Beatrice spoke again.

"Mother. There's nothing here to be concerned about. Alison's fine."

"Very well." She nodded, then brushed by him to mount the stairs.

Kasey looked down at Alison, who was watching her grandmother's retreating back. "I'm sorry, Uncle Jordan. I didn't know Grandmother would be upset. She wasn't here when we left, and we told Millicent, in case you wondered where we were."

"You haven't done anything." He bent and kissed her cheek. "Your grandmother's probably a bit tired after her luncheon today, that's all. She needs to rest awhile. Why don't you take these packages up for Kasey?"

Alison gathered up boxes. "I'll bring wrapping paper to your room."

"Thanks." Children spring back quickly, she noted. Alison was already more concerned with the presents than with her grandmother's annoyance.

Jordan put his hands on Kasey's shoulders as Alison disappeared up the steps. "Shall I apologize, too?" he asked quietly as he soothed the remaining tension from her muscles.

Kasey shook her head. "No." She sighed. She was aware

that it was Beatrice's dislike of her that had caused the confrontation. She felt responsible. "I've put you in a bad position. Alison, too. I never meant to, Jordan."

"Let me handle my mother," he told her. "I've been doing it for a long time. And next time you go off for an afternoon," he added, "invite me. I might have found tramping through shops and a hamburger appealing."

"All right." She smiled, steadying. "Next time I will."

He started to pull her close, then stopped. His brows drew together. "Chocolate cookies?"

CHAPTER ELEVEN

KASEY PAUSED IN THE DRAWING ROOM DOORWAY. She'd taken her time dressing for the dance at Jordan's club, wanting to be certain Beatrice was gone before she came downstairs.

Standing there, she had a moment to study Jordan unobserved as he mixed drinks at the bar. Formal dress—the stark black and white, the perfect tailoring—suited him. He moves well, she thought, a man used to elegant clothes and elegant rooms. Yet there's so much more to him than I realized that first night I walked in here. More depth, more character, more strength. If I could have chosen a man to fall in love with, I couldn't have chosen any better.

Taking a deep breath, she walked into the room. "It seems my timing's perfect."

Jordan turned to watch her. The dress was dark green and clinging with a deep slash of a neckline. It was caught at the side of her waist and fell straight, leaving a slit that opened and closed as she walked.

"I thought once you were a witch," Jordan murmured. "Now I'm sure of it."

Kasey took the glass from his hand. "Like it?" She smiled and sipped. "Jordan, you've picked up the knack for mixing these. You could make a living from it."

"Yes, I like it." He took the glass from her, set it down and then drew her into his arms. He gave her a long, deep, satisfying kiss that begged for more. "The thought comes into my mind," he said as his lips grazed her cheekbone, "of locking those doors over there and staying right where I am."

"Oh, no." Kasey smiled and shook her head. "You asked me for a date. I'm holding you to it."

"We could be late." He kissed her again, lingeringly. They hadn't had nearly enough time together since they had returned from New York. "We've been late before."

But not here, she thought, floating under the kiss. We're not alone here.

She drew herself carefully out of his arms. "Someone

once told me that being late was rude. Besides"—she picked up her glass again—"you promised to dance with me. I should think you dance very well."

It occurred to him that he wasn't going to like sharing her. He shook off the notion. Jealousy was foreign to him. "All right," he agreed. "A date's a date."

Kasey took his hand as they walked to the door. "Can we go parking afterward?" she asked.

"Love to." He grinned and nudged her outside.

⋘⊙⋙

JORDAN SLIPPED TWO GLASSES FROM THE TRAY OF A roving waiter. "Champagne?" he asked her.

"Absolutely." Kasey took the glass and sipped. "It's beautiful here. I'm glad you asked me to come."

He touched the rim of his glass to hers. "To anthropology," he murmured. "A fascinating science."

Kasey gave a low laugh and raised her glass to her lips. She turned to watch a slim brunette in a filmy white dress weave through the crowd toward them. Reaching Jordan, she rose on her toes to kiss his cheek.

"Jordan. You've finally come out of hibernation."

"Hello, Liz. You look lovely, as always."

"I'm surprised you remember what I look like after all

this time. It's been months." She smiled and turned to Kasey. She had round fawn's eyes and creamy skin. There was a single, perfect diamond on a chain at her throat.

"Kathleen Wyatt." Jordan touched Kasey's shoulder lightly. "Elizabeth Bentley."

"Kathleen Wyatt?" Liz repeated. "The name's very familiar, but we haven't met before, have we?"

"No, Miss Bentley, we haven't met." Kasey gave her a friendly smile, appreciating the frank interest in her eyes. "Would you like some champagne?" she asked, slipping a glass from another tray. "It's really very good."

"Thank you." Liz glanced down at the glass, then back at Kasey.

"Kasey's been working with me on my novel," Jordan explained. He could see Liz was both confused and intrigued.

"Oh, yes." A piece fell into place. "Harry Rhodes mentioned your name at dinner the other night." She hesitated a moment. "He said you were extraordinarily intelligent."

"That's because I hustled him at pool." Kasey's eyes gleamed with laughter over the rim of her glass as she lifted it again. "Do you play?"

"Play—pool?" Liz shook her head, and a faint line of concentration appeared between her brows. "No. You're an archaeologist?"

"No, an anthropologist." Kasey smiled and couldn't resist. "An archaeologist is one who studies the life and culture of ancient peoples by excavating ancient cities, relics, artifacts. An anthropologist is one who studies the races, physical and mental characteristics, distributions, customs, social relationships of mankind." She took another sip of champagne. "That's a terrific dress," she commented, nodding at Liz. "French?"

⌒⊙⌒

"YOU DID A FINE JOB OF CONFUSING LIZ," JORDAN stated when he had Kasey in his arms on the dance floor.

"Really?" Kasey lifted her cheek from his shoulder. She laughed at the wry look he gave her. "She's a very pretty lady, Jordan, and a very nice one. I like her."

"You make up your mind quickly."

"Usually it saves time." She smiled as he whirled her around the floor. "I decided you were a marvelous dancer," she pointed out. "And I was right."

"If I told you I'd never enjoyed a waltz more, would you believe me?"

"I might." She laughed up at him.

"I'm going to have to let you dance with the men here who can't keep their eyes off you. I'm not going to like it."

Her brows lifted. "Are there many?" she asked, teasing him while she tried to sort out how she felt about his statement.

"Too many. You walk into a room, and every eye rests on you. Including mine."

Kasey laughed and shook her head. "You've a writer's imagination, Jordan."

"And a man's," he murmured. "I can't get you out of my mind."

She was staring up at him, forgetting the music they moved to, the people who moved with them. "Do you want to?"

He couldn't look away from her. "I don't know." He couldn't think straight when she was in his arms, pressed close. "I wish I did. Is it enough to tell you there's never been another woman who's been as important to me as you are?"

It was a cautious step, and Kasey took it no further. She touched his cheek with her fingers. "It's enough, Jordan."

Throughout the evening Kasey was never alone. She sparked interest everywhere she went. She enjoyed answering the questions put to her and fielding flirtations. She enjoyed the elegance, the glamour, just as she enjoyed a trip to the corner movie. Buttered popcorn or champagne, it was all part of life.

"Miss Wyatt."

Kasey turned away from a discussion with a yachting enthusiast and his wife and smiled at Harry Rhodes. "Hello, Harry. It's good to see you."

"It's nice seeing you again. You look lovely."

"So do you." She touched the lapel of his dinner jacket. He cleared his throat.

"I wanted to tell you how much I enjoyed reading the book you loaned me."

"Anytime, Harry." He had a nice face, she thought. Jordan was fortunate to have him for a friend.

"I've been practicing, you know. I'm going to challenge you to another game of pool."

"I'd like that." She grinned now. "We'll have to try eight ball this time."

"Miss Wyatt . . . Kathleen . . . Kasey," he decided, as her smile warmed for him. "That's what Jordan calls you, isn't it?"

"All my friends do."

He fiddled with his glasses and smiled. His eyes were kind, she thought, like the wise little bear he reminded her of.

"Kasey, I don't suppose you'd care to risk the dance floor with a doddering old professor."

"I don't see one." Kasey set down her glass and offered her hand. "But I'd love to dance with you, Harry."

"Jordan's a very fortunate man to have found you," he told her as they headed for the dance floor.

"But it was *you* who found me, wasn't it, Harry?"

"Then I should pat myself on the back." He liked the dimple at the corner of her mouth, the way her hair curled without design around her face. She seemed a little of the waif, a little of the siren. "I hope Jordan appreciates you."

"He's a very kind man, isn't he? Kind, loving and gentle."

"He loved his brother very much, you know." Harry gave a sigh. "They were close. Allen, his father, was a dear friend of mine. He died several years before, and Beatrice has never been a maternal woman. Best hostess I know," he added. "But simply not cut out for mothering. The boys were quite a pair. A bit wild now and then, but—"

"Wild?" Kasey interrupted with a surprised laugh. "Jordan?"

"He had his moments, my dear." Recalling a few, Harry decided it would be more discreet not to detail them. "It was very difficult for Jordan when he lost his brother. They were twins."

"I didn't know." Losing a brother would be hard enough, she mused, but losing a twin would be losing part of yourself. "He's never talked about it with me."

"He closed himself in after that. It hasn't been until

recently that I've noticed the door opening again." Harry looked down at Kasey. "That's your doing. You care for him very much, don't you?"

Kasey met his eyes directly. "I'm in love with him."

Harry nodded. He was no longer surprised by her frankness. "He's needed someone like you to snap the life back in him. If he's not careful, he could turn out to be a crusty old bachelor like me."

"You're a beautiful man, Harry." The music stopped, and Kasey kissed his cheek, holding him a moment.

"What's this?" Jordan crossed over to them and slipped an arm around Kasey's shoulders. "Turn my back for a moment and you're nuzzling up to my date. I thought I could trust you, Harry."

Harry colored and harrumphed. "Not with this lady, my boy. I'm part of the competition. And I haven't lost my touch yet," he announced before he strolled away.

"What did you do to him?" Bemused, Jordan watched Harry's swagger. "I believe he meant that."

"I certainly hope so." Kasey drew Jordan's eyes back to her. "Would you be jealous? That would be a marvelous Christmas present, Jordan."

"It's not Christmas yet," he countered. "Let's go outside before I have to compete with someone else."

"Competition's very healthy," Kasey stated as they slipped through the terrace doors. "In studies with white mice—"

He kissed her firmly, cutting off the impending lecture. "I'm damned if I'm going to compete with white mice," he muttered, pulling her closer.

His hand was in her hair, and his mouth demanded. Kasey yielded, sensing it was what he needed. Her mouth was soft, and her arms lifted to wind around his neck. A submission of the moment; later there would be time for challenge, for aggression, for equal strength. He needed something different from her now. It was simple to surrender to him when she knew her own power. She could feel his heart pound as he kept her molded against him.

Jordan drew her away to stare down at her. "Who are you?" he muttered. "I never know who you are."

"You're closer to knowing than most," she murmured and turned to lean on the rail. "It's lovely here, Jordan. The air's soft, and I can smell—verbena, I think." Kasey lifted her face. "The stars are close." She sighed and scanned them. "Back at home I used to sit outside for hours and pick out constellations. Pop bought me a telescope one year. I was going to be the first woman on the moon."

"What changed your mind?" There was a click from his lighter, then the scent of tobacco on the air.

Kasey shrugged her shoulders. She would remember that scent for the rest of her life. "I tried to live on dehydrated food for a week. It's terrible." He laughed, and she pointed skyward. "There's Pegasus. See? He flies straight up. Andromeda's head touches his wing." She brought her hand down and sighed. She felt pleasantly sleepy. "Marvelous, isn't it? All the pictures up there. It's comforting knowing they'll be there tomorrow."

Jordan came closer to touch her shoulder. Her skin was smooth and just a bit cool from the night air. "Is that why you dig into the past? Because it's a link with the future?"

She gave another restless shrug. "Maybe."

He tossed aside the cigar and pulled her close again. She rested her head on his shoulder. "Dance with me again, Jordan," she murmured. "The night's almost over."

CHAPTER TWELVE

CHRISTMAS EVE. MAGIC. KASEY WAS READY FOR magic. She had palm trees rather than snow, but she'd lived through Christmases without snow before. This time she had something of more value. She would have the day with the man she loved and with a child who was burning with excitement. That was magic enough for her.

She was aware that her job was finished, or at least nearly so. Jordan spent more and more time working without her. What she filled in now could be done by a letter or a simple phone call. She was procrastinating, and she knew, whether Jordan realized it or not, that he was too. The break had to come—but not on Christmas. Kasey was taking that for herself. When the holidays were over, she'd make her plans, pack, then tell him. In that order. It would be better if everything was set before the words were said.

With a firm plan in mind, Kasey felt better. She told herself she was entitled to a week. The first of the year, she would take the step away from him, away from Alison, and begin again. She was strong; she'd lived through losses before. But now it was Christmas, and she had a family, if only for another week.

She sat on the rug in the drawing room and watched Alison poke at the stacks of presents under the tree. She chattered like a magpie. What might this be? What that *had* to be. How many hours were left?

"Not quite one less than the last time you asked," Jordan told her and pulled her up on his lap. "Why don't we open everything now?"

"Oh, no, Uncle Jordan, we couldn't!" She glanced at Kasey, waiting to be overruled.

"No, we couldn't. Santa would be very annoyed."

Alison laughed and snuggled into the curve of Jordan's arm. "Kasey, you know there isn't really a Santa Claus."

"I know nothing of the sort. You, Miss Taylor, are a cynic."

"I am?" Alison digested the word. Reaching over, she picked up a small glass ball that held a miniature forest scene. Turning it upside down, she let the snow fall. "I haven't seen this before."

"No." Jordan had wondered when she would notice it. "I found it in the attic this morning. It was your father's when we were boys."

"Really?"

"Yes. Really. I thought you might like to have it."

"To keep?" She curled her fingers around the glass and looked up at him.

"To keep."

Alison looked back at the glass and watched the snow drift. "He liked the snow," she mused. "When we lived in Chicago, we had snow fights. He'd let me win." She leaned back against Jordan's chest and tilted the ball again.

Kasey watched them and kept silent. He'd gone searching for that to give Alison something of her father for Christmas. If she hadn't loved him before, she would have fallen in love with him at that moment. He's a good man, she thought. Above everything else he is, he's a good man.

She rose, wanting to give them time alone.

"Kasey?" Jordan's eyes lifted to hers, and she stopped.

"I think I still have a few things to wrap," she told him. He smiled, seeing through her.

"Didn't someone mention something about stringing popcorn?"

"Popcorn?" Alison's eyes lit up. "For the tree?"

"Kasey told me a tree wasn't suitably dressed unless it wore popcorn," Jordan stated. "What do you think?"

"May we do it now?"

"I'm all for it, but Kasey seems to have something else to do." Jordan kept his eyes on her, still smiling.

"I'm flexible," Kasey returned, then looked at Alison. "We'll need several miles of string and three needles. Can you handle it?"

"Are we going to eat some, too?"

"Absolutely."

Alison scrambled up and, taking the glass ball with her, shot out of the room.

"Sometimes you're transparent, Kasey." Jordan rose and went to her. "You were going to cry and didn't want to do it in front of Alison. Or in front of me."

"That was a marvelous thing you did."

"Alison was with me last Christmas, and it never occurred to me." He lifted Kasey's chin a bit higher and kissed her.

"Don't make me cry, Jordan. It's Christmas Eve."

"I've got them!" Alison came to the doorway at a full run. She held up a packet of needles and a thick ball of string.

"Half the battle." Kasey crossed to her, then turned back to Jordan. "Coming?"

"I wouldn't miss it."

As they approached the kitchen door, Jordan said, "You know, I'm not sure how Francois is going to take this. His kitchen's sacred."

"Piece of cake," Kasey murmured as they entered.

Francois turned and bowed. He didn't wear the white hat Kasey had hoped for all those weeks ago, but he did have the moustache. *"Monsieur."* He bowed at Jordan. "May I assist you?"

"Francois." Jordan took a moment. He'd witnessed more than one tantrum over the years. "We have a need to make something for the Christmas tree."

"Oui, monsieur?"

"We're going to string popcorn."

"Popcorn? You want to make this popcorn in my kitchen?" Before Jordan could answer, Francois was off on a stream of indignant French.

"Francois?"

He turned and gave a stiff bow. *"Mademoiselle?"*

Kasey smiled at him. *"Vôtre cuisine est magnifique,"* she began, then continued in flawless French. She praised his food, his stove, his counters, sampled from the stockpot he had simmering while he joined the discussion with passion. She was enthusiastic about the perfection of his cookware and impressed with his cutlery.

When she had finished, he kissed her hand cordially, bowed to Jordan again and strolled from the room.

"Well." Jordan glanced at the closed door, then back at Kasey. He watched as she took down a pan and placed it on the stove. "Where did you learn to speak French like that?"

"My roommate at college was a language major. Where's the popcorn?"

He walked to her, ignoring the question. "What did you say to him? I always thought my French was good, but the two of you went well beyond me."

"Just this and that." Kasey smiled. "I did tell him you wanted him and the rest of the kitchen staff to have the night off. You do have popcorn, don't you?"

Jordan laughed and reached into a bottom cabinet. "I smuggled it in at great personal risk."

"You're a tough guy, Taylor." She took the can from him. "I'll need some oil." He gestured for Alison to get it, then leaned close and whispered a quick French phrase in Kasey's ear. Her mouth turned up. "I'm shocked," she murmured. "Interested, but shocked. I don't think I'll ask you where you learned that."

In moments the kitchen was noisy with the popping of the corn. Alison sat at the butcher block table, ankles crossed, carefully cutting lengths of string. Jordan settled across from her and watched. When was the last time he had sat listening to that sound? he wondered. In college? No, at his brother's house, five, perhaps six, years ago. Perhaps Kasey had been right. He had insulated himself.

"Another masterpiece," Kasey declared, turning the popcorn into a bowl. "No duds."

He dipped his hand into the bowl. "Where's the butter?" he demanded. Alison's hand brushed his as she dug in.

"Grab a needle," Kasey instructed each of them.

They worked in anything but silence. Alison chattered continually between mouthfuls. Her string of popcorn grew longer by the minute. It seemed to Kasey that they had sat like this before on other Christmas Eves, that they would sit like this again. But she knew better and shivered.

"Cold?" Jordan asked her.

"No." She tried to shake off the feeling. "A goat ran over my grave."

"That's a goose," he said and smiled at her.

"Goose, goat." She shrugged. She stuffed a piece of popcorn into her mouth. "You're not doing so well there, Jordan," she observed.

"I need incentive."

"Mine's going to be the longest," Alison declared. "It's going to be a hundred miles long."

"Don't count your chickens before they cross the road," Kasey advised. "How do you do that, Jordan?" she asked, studying him. "Did it come naturally, or did you practice?"

Jordan shook his head in amused confusion.

"I mean lift one eyebrow," Kasey explained. "It's marvelous. I'd love to be able to do it, but both of mine work at the same time. Let's have some hot chocolate." She sprang up and began to rummage through cupboards. Jordan abandoned his string and watched her.

"Kasey, come here a minute."

"Jordan, preparing hot chocolate requires concentration and care." She measured in the milk. Crossing the room, he took her arm and pulled her under the doorway. He pointed above their heads with one finger. Kasey smiled at the mistletoe. "Is it real?" she asked.

"It's real," he assured her.

"Well, in that case . . ." She touched her mouth lightly to his.

"That's not how they kiss in the movies," Alison commented and plucked another piece of popcorn.

"Absolutely right," Jordan agreed before Kasey could

comment. He drew her back into his arms and covered her mouth with his. The kiss lengthened, and the sweetness of it made Kasey's throat ache. She held him close. She would remember that kiss before all the others, she knew.

"That was much better," Alison stated when Kasey drew away. "My string's finished."

Later they sat in the drawing room again. Alison was curled next to Jordan on the sofa with Kasey's guitar in her lap. Kasey watched the colors from the lights on the tree play across her face as she drifted into sleep.

"She's had a long day," Kasey murmured.

"I'm looking forward to seeing her face when she gets her presents tomorrow." He slipped the guitar from Alison's limp arms and handed it to Kasey. "Your little gift is safely tucked away?"

"Charles is guarding my little gift in the garage. I'm not sure he's going to part with it easily." She rose. "I'll take Alison up and put her to bed."

"I'll do it." Jordan shifted his niece into his arms and stood. "Why don't you put some music on?"

When he had gone, Kasey went to the cabinet that held the stereo. Chopin, she decided, sifting through the albums. It was a night for romance.

The house was quiet. The servants were settled in their

wing. Beatrice was at a party. It might have been only the three of them in the house. Kasey sighed as she slipped the record onto the turntable. For tonight she could pretend it was true. Wandering to the window, she parted the curtains and looked out. The moon was high and full, the night clear. She found Pegasus again and mused over it. When she heard the doors shut quietly, she turned. Kasey watched Jordan lock them.

"Did you settle her in all right?" Her heart began to skip rapidly. Silly, she thought. I act as though it's the first time I've been with him.

"She's fine. She never even woke up. You sleep like that." He crossed the room and set the bottle of wine he carried on the bar. "Deep, like a child." He opened the wine, then moved to the fireplace. Kneeling, he set gas flames burning over the logs. "Now you can pretend it's snowing." He smiled up at her.

"You do see through me, don't you?"

"At times." When he had poured two glasses, he moved back in front of the fire and sat. He held up a hand for her. Kasey took it and settled next to him. "How do you feel?" he asked when she was leaning against him.

"Like I'm snowed in," she murmured, accepting the wine

he offered. "Snuggled in a log cabin in the Adirondacks, away from the world and its problems."

"Is there room in the log cabin for me?"

She tilted her head to smile at him. "Anytime."

"We'd have wood," he said quietly, and he took the glass from her hand. "And wine." He bent to kiss the corner of her mouth. "And each other." Gently he lowered her to the floor. "We wouldn't need anything else."

"No." Kasey's lids lowered as she drew him closer. "Nothing else."

She lost herself in the feel of him, in the taste of him. Her mind and body were in complete harmony, and both belonged to him. From somewhere deep in the center of the house, the clock struck midnight, and it was Christmas.

How long they loved each other that night Kasey would never know. Neither of them had wanted to unlock the door and open themselves to the rest of the world. Once, when they dozed together, Jordan woke to hear the front door open and close behind his mother. Then the house was silent again. Theirs. He turned to Kasey and roused her slowly until she was quivering for him again and he for her. There was firelight and the colors from the tree and the scent of pine. The wine grew warm.

Kasey slept again and woke groggily when Jordan lifted her.

"I'll take you up," he murmured.

"I don't want to leave you." She buried her face in his neck. "The nights are too short. Hours and hours too short."

Then she was asleep again, as deeply as Alison had been when he had carried her up the stairs.

⁂

MORNING CAME ALL TOO SOON. ONLY HER OWN DETER-mination and Alison's excitement kept Kasey from crawling back under the covers. The neat, formal drawing room was soon strewn with torn paper, boxes and discarded ribbons. A cocker spaniel puppy, Kasey's gift to Alison, raced around the tree while Alison sat, awestruck, with a new guitar, a gift from her uncle, on her lap.

"Shouldn't you wake your mother, Jordan?" Kasey murmured, pushing some crumpled paper aside.

"At six o'clock in the morning?" He laughed and shook his head. "Mother doesn't rise before ten, Christmas or no Christmas. We'll have a very civilized brunch later."

Kasey wrinkled her nose and grabbed for a box. "It's about time I had one," she announced, knowing the gift was from Alison. "I've heard a lot of whispering about this one," she said, unwinding the ribbon slowly. "Seen a lot of telling looks." Alison caught her bottom lip between her teeth and looked at Jordan. "Like that one," Kasey stated and ripped the paper with a flourish. Opening the box, she found a long pale green neck scarf in soft wool.

"It's the first present I ever made," Alison said anxiously. "Rose, the kitchen maid, taught me. I made some mistakes."

Kasey tried to raise her eyes, tried to speak, but could do neither. She stroked the awkwardly crocheted scarf with her fingers.

"Do you like it?"

Kasey looked up and nodded helplessly. Her eyes were already brimming over.

"Women," Jordan said, tucking Alison's hair behind her ear. "Some women," he corrected, "tend to weep when they're particularly happy. Kasey's one of them."

"Really?"

"Really," Kasey managed and took a deep breath. "Alison, it's the most beautiful present I've ever had." She gathered the girl into her arms and squeezed. "Thank you."

"She really likes it," Alison said, grinning at Jordan over Kasey's shoulder. "Do you think she'll cry if you give her yours?"

"Why don't we find out?" Jordan reached under the tree

for a small, square box. "Of course, maybe she's not interested in any more presents."

"Of course I am." Kasey drew out of Alison's arms. "I'm very greedy on Christmas." She took the box from him and drew a deep breath. Opening it, she felt her heart lurch for the second time that morning.

She held the gold, finely etched drop earrings, remarkably similar to those she had seen the day she had bought his unicorn. She looked up at him and shook her head. "Jordan, how did you remember something like this?"

"I haven't forgotten anything you've told me. I thought this went with it." He handed her another box, this one long and flat, then smiled as she hesitated. "I thought you were greedy on Christmas."

Kasey opened the box and found three thin gold chains ingeniously twisted together to form one. "It's beautiful," she murmured.

He took the chain from her fingers and clasped it around her neck.

Kasey swallowed, then laid her cheek against his. "Thank you, Jordan." She scrambled up. "I'm going to see about some coffee."

"She liked yours, too," Alison told him and shifted her guitar. "She was crying again."

When Millicent brought coffee and croissants into the drawing room fifteen minutes later, she stood balancing the tray and stared. In all her years in the Taylor household she'd never seen anything like it. Papers and ribbons and boxes were everywhere. And Mr. Taylor was wrestling with a puppy in the middle of it all. *Mr. Taylor!* Miss Alison and Miss Wyatt were giggling. No, she'd never seen anything like it, not in this house.

CHAPTER THIRTEEN

K ASEY INTENDED TO KEEP HERSELF VERY BUSY
when she left Palm Springs. First she was going home.
She had made her decision; New Year's Eve would mark her
last full day with Jordan. All she had left to do was tell Jordan. After looking at it from every angle—from hers, from
his, from Alison's—Kasey had decided to wait until the first
of the year. Her flight was booked. It would hurt less if the
hours between weren't heavy with the knowledge that they
were the last ones. She'd cram everything she could into that
final twenty-four hours.

"I'd have had you in the third game of the second set if
I hadn't double-faulted." She swung her racket at the air as
she and Jordan walked from the tennis court. "And if you

hadn't served to my backhand in the fourth game of the second set, I would have won that one, too. You really are a vicious player, coming into the net like that."

He took her racket, a bit leery of the enthusiasm she showed in swinging it. "Look, there's Alison by the pool. She appears to be dutifully doing her homework."

Alison glanced up as they approached, waved, then settled back with a sigh. "Uncle Jordan, I don't know what to do about this assignment."

"No?" He set the rackets down on the umbrellaed table. "What is it?"

"I have to list five items typical of the nineteen eighties. Something I'd put into a time capsule to show future societies what our culture was like."

"Alison." He grinned and ran a finger down her nose. "Why ask a writer when you have an anthropologist?"

"Oh, I forgot." She looked up at Kasey. "What would you put in a time capsule?"

"Let's see." Kasey narrowed her eyes against the sun a moment. "A stalk of wheat, a container of petroleum, an MOS chip, a cassette of punk rock music and a pair of Gucci loafers."

Jordan laughed. "And that's your encapsulation of the eighties?"

Alison frowned as she scribbled. "What's an MOS chip?"

"It's a—"

"Oh, no." Jordan stopped Kasey's explanation cold. "Don't get her started, Alison."

"Well," Alison said, frowning at the list doubtfully, "I suppose I'd better think about this some more." She gave Kasey a look that told her she'd been little help, then left to work out her problem indoors.

"I'm not sure that Alison or her teacher is ready for your opinion on our society," Jordan commented.

"It was my educated analysis of our culture as it stands today, from technology to fashion. You know, Jordan, you really look hot after that tennis match. You should cool off."

She gave him a firm shove and sent him backwards into the pool. He surfaced, pushing his hair from his eyes. "Impulse," she claimed and grabbed her middle as she laughed. "I've never had a firm control over impulses." Saying nothing, he narrowed his eyes and swam to the edge. "Sorry, Jordan, but you really did look hot. I'm sure the water's wonderful. You're not mad, are you? I'll help you out."

She'd no more than offered her hand when she realized her mistake. He took it firmly, then grinned at her as he gave it a quick tug and sent her headlong into the water. She came up sputtering.

"I had that coming, I suppose."

"So you did. How's the water?"

"Terrific." She treaded water with one hand and pulled off a sneaker with the other. "I've always thought"—she tossed the sneaker over his head and out of the pool—"that when you find yourself in an inevitable situation, you should make the most of it." She lofted her other shoe, then, doing a surface dive, streaked along the bottom.

She jerked when Jordan's hands took her waist. He turned her, and she found herself tangled with him in an underwater kiss. Her heartbeat jumped from normal to frantic, and she clung to him. When she surfaced, her pulse was still soaring.

"I was making the most of an inevitable situation," Jordan murmured and caught the lobe of her ear in his teeth.

"You scared me." She took a deep breath. "I should never have seen that shark movie."

"We don't stock sharks in the winter." He ran a hand through her hair. "It's nearly copper when it's wet and the sun hits it. The first day you were here I stood at my window and watched you swim. I couldn't get you out of my mind even then."

She leaned her head on his shoulder. It was so difficult to be strong when he was gentle. She wanted to tell him again that she loved him, that it was breaking her heart to have to leave him. She didn't know, even then, what she would do if he asked her to stay. Or perhaps she did, and that was why she had made her plans without telling him. They couldn't go on as they were, and she saw no future for them. If he could love her . . . But Kasey shook her head and drew away from him.

"I'll race you," she challenged. "I'm a much better swimmer than tennis player."

He smiled. "All right, I'll give you a head start."

Kasey lifted her brows. "That is an assumption of male superiority." She pushed her hair from her eyes. "I'll take it."

She was off like a rocket in a flurry of water. Even with her advantage, Jordan reached the far edge two strokes ahead of her. Kasey wrinkled her nose at him. "Of course," she began and stood in the shallow water, "if I'd grown up in a pool . . ."

She noted that he was paying no attention to her words. Following his eyes, she glanced down.

The T-shirt she had worn modestly enough on the tennis court now clung to her breasts. Rather than a cover, it was an erotic invitation. Her brief shorts were molded wetly to her hips and upper thighs. Naked, she would have been less of a temptation. Water ran slowly down the sleekness of her hair.

"I think this sort of swimming apparel belongs in deeper water," Kasey decided and pushed away from the edge.

She was in his arms before she was halfway across the pool. His mouth took hers, hungry, quickly desperate. They lowered below the surface again, tied to each other. Kasey hung on as a mixture of fear and passion ran through her. There were sensations of weightlessness, of claustrophobia, of helplessness. She might have fought against them, but the will had slipped from her, and she held him tighter. He brought them up, and air rushed into her lungs.

"You're trembling," he noticed abruptly. "Did I frighten you?"

"I don't know." She held on and let him keep them above surface. "Oh, Jordan, I want you," she breathed. The need was unexpectedly urgent and powerful.

His mouth found hers again. His excitement was doubled by the desire he felt pouring out of her. "How long can you hold your breath?" he murmured.

"Not long enough." She gave a shaky laugh and searched for his lips again. "Not nearly long enough. Will we drown?"

"Probably." His hand ran down her side, to her hip, to her thigh and back to her waist. "Do you care?"

"Not at the moment. Just kiss me again. Just kiss me and don't say anything."

She couldn't bear it. By that time the next day she would be on a plane. She wouldn't be able to reach out and touch him, to feel his hands on her. She would have the taste of him only in memory. These three months out of her life would be swallowed up by whatever was to come. How could she leave? How could she stay? Already the price she was going to have to pay seemed overwhelmingly high. Then she'd take something else for the bargain, she thought. One last night. One full, last night.

"Jordan, let's not go to that party tonight." She drew away from him, wanting to see his face. "I need to be alone with you, the way we were in New York. Can't we go someplace, just for tonight? Tomorrow's a whole new year. I want to spend the last night of this one with you. Just you."

"A suite at the Hyatt?" he murmured. "Champagne and caviar? I seem to recall you're rather fond of caviar."

"Yes." Her grip around his neck was quick and desperate as she brought her cheek to his. "Or pizza and beer at the Last Chance Motel. It doesn't matter. I love you." She couldn't stop herself from saying it. "I love you so much." Her mouth fastened on his before he could speak.

"Jordan!"

Beatrice's voice broke through the quiet. Jordan drew his mouth from Kasey's without hurry.

"Mother." He glanced up, keeping an arm around Kasey. "Back so soon?"

"What are you doing?"

"Why, I'm swimming," he told her easily. "And kissing Kasey. Was there something you wanted?"

"You're aware that we have servants who could wander out here at any time?"

"Yes. Was there something else?"

Beatrice's eyes flared, but she kept her dignity. Kasey was forced to admire her for it. "Harry Rhodes phoned. He needs to see you in an hour on business. He says it's quite important."

"All right. Thank you."

"You've made her angry, Jordan," Kasey commented when Beatrice left them.

"I'll probably make her a good deal angrier," he mused. It was time for some changes, he thought. Some definite changes. The house was his inheritance, but it might be wise to turn it over to her and take Alison elsewhere. And Kasey . . . Kasey was something else. Well, they had the whole night to talk about it, he decided and pulled her close again. "If you're ready when I get back from talking to Harry, we can start early."

"Talk fast," Kasey told him.

KASEY HAD JUST DRIED HER HAIR WHEN THE KNOCK came at her bedroom door. "Come in." She opened her closet. The green dress again tonight? she wondered and pulled it out. "Hello, Millicent."

The maid hovered in the doorway. "Miss . . ." Millicent folded her hands in front of her and looked uncomfortable. "Mrs. Taylor would like to see you—in her sitting room."

"Now?" Kasey fingered the material of the dress she held.

"Yes, please."

I might as well get it over with, she thought and hung the dress back in the closet. It was going to be unpleasant. If she hadn't known it already, the maid's face told everything.

"All right, I'll go right now."

Millicent cleared her throat. "I'm to take you."

Kasey sighed. She could hardly blame the maid. "Lead on," she invited, and followed her.

Millicent knocked on Beatrice's door, turned the knob, then hurried away. Kasey took one last deep breath and entered.

"Mrs. Taylor?"

"Come in, Miss Wyatt." Beatrice never turned from her ivory-toned desk. "And shut the door."

Kasey obeyed and found herself itching for a cigarette. The room was oppressive and, she thought, as difficult to live with as the woman. "What can I do for you, Mrs. Taylor?"

"Sit down, Miss Wyatt." She waved her hand toward an Edwardian chair. "It's time we had a chat."

Kasey seated herself and awaited the inevitable.

"You've stretched your time here as far as possible." Beatrice turned to her now and folded her hands on the desk.

"Are you concerned with Jordan's research, Mrs. Taylor?" You can't hurt me today, she told herself. It's my last one. "Why don't you tell me just what's on your mind, Mrs. Taylor, and spare us both," she said aloud.

"I've checked your credentials." Beatrice tapped a gold pen against the desk. It was her only outward sign of emotion. "You seem to be considered an expert in your field."

"You checked up on me." Kasey could feel the anger rising and tried to stem it.

"In doing so, I learned you're Samuel Wyatt's granddaughter. I'm slightly acquainted with his daughter, your aunt. There was quite a scandal years back concerning you. A very unfortunate affair." She tapped the pen again. "A pity you didn't stay with your aunt rather than being raised by your grandfather."

"Please." Kasey's voice had lowered. "Don't make me angry."

Beatrice noted she had cracked Kasey's calm. That had been her first objective. "You weren't in your paternal grandfather's will."

"You have done your share of checking."

"I'm a very thorough woman, Miss Wyatt."

"But not one to quickly come to the point."

"The point, then," Beatrice agreed. "Apparently you're financially solvent but hardly . . ."

"Loaded?" Kasey suggested.

"In your vernacular," Beatrice conceded. "Your stay here has been a very lucrative arrangement for you. It's quite understandable that you would pursue the possibilities of future rewards by ingratiating yourself with Jordan and with Alison."

"Future rewards?" Kasey felt the burning start in the pit of her stomach.

"I didn't think I'd need to be graphic." Beatrice set down the pen and folded her hands again. "Jordan is a very wealthy man. Alison will come into a very healthy inheritance at maturity."

"I see." Kasey struggled to keep her hands still. "You're implying that I hope to benefit financially by developing a relationship with Jordan and Alison." She gave Beatrice a long, level look. "You're a hard lady, Mrs. Taylor. Doesn't it occur to you that I'd care about them regardless of the size of their bankbooks?"

"No." Beatrice let the word hang a moment. "I've dealt with your type before. Alison's mother was one, but my son wouldn't listen. He chose to marry her over my objections and move halfway across the country. Of course," she said as she sat back and eyed Kasey, "the problem is different in this case. Jordan has no intention of marrying you. He's satisfied with an affair. Again, in your vernacular, you over-played your hand."

Kasey wanted to throw something. She wanted to rip some holes in the perfection of white that surrounded her. She sat rigid with control. "I'm aware of the boundaries of my relationship with Jordan, Mrs. Taylor. I always have been. You don't have anything to worry about."

"I'm not going to tolerate you under my roof any longer. Your influence on Alison will take months to repair."

"A lifetime, I hope." Kasey rose. She had to get out of that room. "You're never going to fit her into that mold again. She's outgrown it."

"Jordan has custody of Alison."

It was the tone, not the words, that halted Kasey. She felt a quick thrill of fear. "Yes."

Beatrice turned a bit in her chair so she might face Kasey directly. "If you don't leave today, this afternoon, I'll be forced, for Alison's sake, to sue him for custody of her."

"That's absurd." The fear came back, doubled in force. She felt the cold hit her skin. "No court would give you custody over Jordan."

"Perhaps, perhaps not." Beatrice moved her shoulders elegantly. "But you know how distressing a court battle can be, particularly when there's a child involved. Suing on the grounds of immoral conduct would make it rather unpleasant."

"He's your son." The words came out as barely a whisper. "You couldn't do that to him. To Alison. Jordan's done nothing to hurt her; he never would."

"Alison requires protection." She gave Kasey a cool glance. "So does Jordan."

"Protection? You mean manipulation, don't you?" She crossed back to Beatrice. She had to be dreaming. But not even her nightmare hurt this acutely. "You wouldn't do this to them. You couldn't. She's just a child. She loves him." She wouldn't cry in front of this woman. "You don't have anything to gain from this. You don't love Alison the way Jordan does. You don't need her. If you could understand what it's like to be fought over this way, you wouldn't do it."

Beatrice took a small breath. "The choice is up to you."

It was incredible, impossible, but Kasey saw she meant every word she said. "I was going tomorrow," she said quietly. "I'm not worth it, Mrs. Taylor."

"Today, before Jordan returns. You're to say nothing of this to him."

"Today," Kasey agreed. There were tears in her voice; she

couldn't prevent them. She struggled to keep them from her eyes. "Today, because I'm capable of something you're not. Of loving them both enough to give them what they need. Each other."

Beatrice turned her back again. "Millicent will have your bags packed by now, and Charles will drive you wherever you'd like to go." She opened her checkbook. "I'm willing to compensate you for your discretion and for your inconvenience, Miss Wyatt—"

Kasey's hand slammed down on the checkbook and cut her off. Beatrice looked up in surprise.

"Don't press your luck," Kasey whispered. "I gave you my word. It's free." She lifted her hand slowly and straightened. "There'll come a time when you'll have to deal with what you did today. You've lost more than I ever had, Mrs. Taylor."

She made it out the door, then nearly doubled over with the pain. She needed time, a few moments, to pull herself back together. She still had to see Alison. She wouldn't leave without saying good-bye to her. Let me find the right words. Kasey moved down the hall like a sleepwalker. Don't let me cry in front of Alison.

The sharp flash of pain had left her numb. She reached for the knob of Alison's door with nerveless fingers.

"Kasey!" Alison glanced up. The puppy was curled on

the bedspread while Alison sat with him plucking at her guitar. "I learned a new song. Shall I play it for you?"

"Alison." Kasey came to sit beside her.

"What's wrong?" The child's forehead creased as she studied Kasey. "You look funny."

"Alison. You remember I told you that someday I'd have to go." She saw the look in the child's eyes and touched her cheek. "It's someday, Alison."

"No." She set the guitar aside and grabbed Kasey's hand. "You don't have to. You could stay."

"I explained it to you before. Remember? About my job?"

"You don't want to stay?" The tears were starting. Kasey felt a moment of panic.

"Alison, it's not a matter of wanting. I can't."

"You could. You could if you wanted to."

"Alison, look at me." Kasey was on the edge and knew it. But there was no leaving her this way. "Sometimes people can't do exactly what they want. I love you, Alison, but I have to go."

"What will I do?" It was almost a wail as she threw her arms around Kasey's neck.

"You have Jordan. And I'll write you, I promise. Maybe in the summer you can visit. Like we talked about before."

"The summer's months and months away."

Kasey hugged her tight, then drew her back. "Sometimes time goes quickly." She slipped the gold band from her finger and pressed it into Alison's hand. "This is for you. Whenever you think I don't love you anymore, you can look at it and remember I do." Rising, she walked to the doorway. The pain was festering, and her time was running out.

"Alison . . ." She turned back with her hand on the knob. "Tell Jordan I . . ." She shook her head and opened the door. "Just take care of him for me."

ᥱᥫᥰᥰ

THERE WAS ONLY ONE SMALL LIGHT ON IN HER HOTEL room, but even that hurt her eyes. Kasey couldn't summon the energy to walk over and switch it off. The weeping had drained her, left her sick and empty. She could hear the sounds of celebration from other rooms.

It was nearly midnight.

I should be with him now, Kasey thought. I should have had this one last night. What did he think when he came back and found me gone? Gone without a word. He'll never understand. He can't ever understand, she reminded herself. Will he be hurt or just angry? She shook her head. It was no use speculating. It was over.

She heard the rattle of a key and turned. When Jordan walked in, she said nothing. Her thoughts were drowned in pain and shock.

"You should use a chain when you want to shut someone out, Kasey." He tossed the key onto a table. "Keys are easy enough to come by. Twenty dollars and a good story buys one. You know all about good stories."

She sat exactly where she was. Beatrice's threat cut off her impulse to run into his arms. "How did you find me?"

"Charles." He turned and fastened the chain. "Though I had to visit a few bars to find him. He had the night off."

"You seem to have put the time to good use." He'd been drinking, she noted, if not heavily, enough to show. She had to keep calm. Her hands were beginning to shake, and she curled her fingers around the edge of the dresser behind her.

Jordan glanced around the small hotel room. "You didn't choose the Hyatt, I see."

"No." There were going to be angry words, hard words. Kasey rose and reached for a cigarette. "Isn't that ridiculous? Hotels are always leaving matches everywhere, and I can't find one." She caught her breath when he gripped her arms and spun her around.

"Why did you leave?"

"I had to leave sometime, Jordan." Her voice tightened with pain as his fingers dug into her skin. "We both know the research was finished."

"Research?" If he didn't keep his fingers tight, he was afraid he'd strike her. She'd hurt him more than he had known he could be hurt. She had opened him up for the pain. He gave her a savage shake. "Is that all there is between us?"

She was beginning to tremble all over, but he didn't seem to notice. She had never seen him like this—brutal, furious. She wished he would hit her if that would bring a quick end to it.

"Damn you." He shook her again, nearly lifting her off her feet. "Couldn't you at least have faced me with it? Did you have to leave behind my back, without a word?"

Kasey gripped the dresser edge again. The sickness was rising back to her throat. "It's better this way, Jordan. I—"

"Better?" The word exploded from him. Kasey jumped. "For whom? If you didn't have the decency to think of me, what about Alison?"

That was almost too much to bear. Kasey closed her eyes a moment. "I thought of Alison, Jordan. You must believe I thought of Alison."

"How can I believe anything you say? She was devastated. Look at me." He took her hair and pulled her head back. "I spent an hour holding her while she cried, trying to make her understand what I couldn't."

"I did what I had to do." Her head was beginning to spin. She had to make him leave, and quickly. "Jordan, you've had too much to drink." Her voice was amazingly calm now. "And you're hurting me. I want you to go."

"You said you loved me."

Kasey swallowed and straightened. "I changed my mind." She watched the color drain from his face.

"Changed your mind?" The words came slowly, with no understanding.

"That's right. Now go and leave me alone. I've a plane to catch in the morning."

"Bitch." He whispered the word as he dragged her against him. "I'll go when I'm finished. We still have a date."

"No." She struggled against him in quick panic. "No, Jordan."

"We'll finish what you started," he told her. "Here. Now."

And his mouth was on hers, cutting off her protest. Kasey pushed against him, wild with fear. Would even this be taken from her—the memories of the joy of loving him, being loved by him. He was dragging her toward the bed, and she fought, but he was strong and senseless with rage. What are we doing to each other? Her mind dimmed as he ripped the shirt from her shoulders. His hands were everywhere, pulling, tearing her clothes as she struggled against him.

The memory of Beatrice's calm, cool face floated behind her eyes. I won't let you do this to us.

Kasey stopped struggling. Under Jordan's mouth, hers softened and surrendered. I can give you this, she told him silently and felt her panic subside. One last night. She hasn't taken it from us, after all. She stopped thinking and let herself love.

CHAPTER FOURTEEN

K ASEY AWOKE TO FULL, BLINDING LIGHT. SHE moaned in automatic protest and rolled over. Her hand touched the emptiness beside her. She opened her eyes. He was gone. She struggled to sit up, scanning the room quickly for some sign of Jordan. When she laid her hand on the pillow beside hers, she found it cool.

When had he gone? She remembered only that they had loved each other again and again in the night, in desperation and in silence. She thought he had slept, was certain they had had a few hours of total peace together. She needed to know they had.

No one could take those last hours from her. If there hadn't been tenderness, there had been need. He won't hurt

---

anymore. Her last hope was that the night would have purged the pain from him, if not his anger. She doubted Jordan would ever forgive her for her method of ending it. Kasey rose from the bed. She still had a plane to catch.

When she saw the note on the dresser, she stared at it. It might be better not to read it, to pretend she hadn't seen it. What could he say to her now that wouldn't bring the pain flooding back? But she reached for it before she could stop herself. She opened it and read:

Kasey,

An apology for last night would mean little, but I have nothing else to offer. Anger is no excuse for what happened. I can only tell you I regret it more than anything I've ever done.

I'm leaving you a check for your services of the last month. I hope you realize what you've given me, because I don't have the words to tell you.

Jordan

Kasey read the letter through once, then again. She'd been right to think it would bring pain. She crumpled it in her hand, then dropped it on the floor. Regret it, she thought and slowly picked up the check that had been laid beneath the note. She was cold now. She had little emotion left to spend. Briskly she scanned the amount and gave a quick laugh.

"Generous, Jordan. You're a generous man." She tore the check methodically into tiny pieces and let them drift to the floor. "That ought to drive your accountant crazy." She wasn't going to cry again. There weren't any tears left. With a shuddering sigh, Kasey reached for a cigarette.

"Montana," she decided all at once. "Montana will have six feet of snow and be cold as hell." Now wasn't the time to go home, she thought. It would be too easy to fall apart at home. Dashing to the phone, Kasey prepared to change her plans.

ॐ

DR. EDWARD BRENNAN SWITCHED OFF THE IGNITION ON his old Pontiac. The sun was beginning to set, and he'd put in a full day. His back let him know it. Getting old, he mused as he sat. There'd been a day when he could have delivered three babies, plucked out a pair of tonsils, set a broken tibia and inoculated three families against the flu before lunch without slackening speed. But he was seventy and thinking it was time to slow down.

Maybe it was time to take on an associate, someone young with fresh ideas. Dr. Brennan liked fresh ideas. He smiled a moment and watched the sunset. Too bad Kasey hadn't taken to medicine. She'd have made a hell of a doctor. What a bedside manner she would have had.

There were orange streaks shooting through the trees on his mountain. He was very proprietary about his little section of land. His mountain, his sunset. He felt that way when he sat alone. It was a good feeling and kept him going.

Opening the car door, he lifted out the bundle of homemade bread and preserves that Mrs. Oates had pressed on him when he had treated her boy for chicken pox. He would enjoy his fee with a cup of coffee. After, he thought as he stretched his tired back, he might just have a glass of the illegal whiskey Mr. Oates had slipped him before he had left. Oates had the best still on the east side of the mountain.

The door to his house was never locked, and he pushed it open, already tasting the bread.

"Hello, Pop."

Dr. Brennan jolted, then stared at the woman seated behind his kitchen table. *"Kasey!"* He was stunned to find her and surprised that she hadn't jumped up to rush to him for a fierce hug and noisy kiss. It was her traditional way of greeting him, whether they had been parted for a day or a year. "I thought you were still in Tennessee."

"Nope, I'm right here." She smiled at him, then glanced at the bundle he carried. "Smells like fresh bread. Part of your fee?"

"Mrs. Oates," he answered, crossing the room to set the bundle on the table.

"Ah." Kasey grinned up at him. "Then you'll have something a little more lively from Mr. Oates, I imagine. How's your stomach lining?"

"Sturdy enough for a glass or two."

She laid a hand on his. "How are you, Pop?"

"Fine, Kasey." He was studying her face carefully with a mixture of affection and professionalism. Something was not quite right. He squeezed her hand in return. She'd tell him when she was ready, in her own way. He'd known her too long to expect anything else. "What about you? What have you been up to? I haven't had one of your six-page letters in nearly a month."

"Not too much." She gave a half shrug. "I spent a couple of weeks in Montana. I got a terrific coat there; it would keep you warm in the Aleutians. I joined the Phiefer team for a while in Utah. Molly Phiefer's just as tough as ever. She celebrated her sixty-eighth birthday in camp. I did a two-part lecture in St. Paul and fished for trout in Tennessee. And I quit smoking." Her eyes darkened. She drew in her breath. "Pop . . . I'm pregnant."

"Pregnant?" His eyes shot open. "What do you mean, pregnant?"

"Pop." Kasey reached for his hand. "You're a doctor. You know what pregnant means."

"Kasey." Dr. Brennan discovered he had to sit down. "How did it happen?"

"The traditional way," she said, attempting a smile. "Even modern methods aren't always reliable," she added, anticipating the inevitable question.

He'd let that pass for now. "How far along are you?"

"What's today?"

He was used to her casual indifference to the passing of time. "May seventeenth."

"Four months and seventeen days."

"Very specific," he noted with a nod of his head.

"I'm sure." She laced and unlaced her hands.

Observing the nervous move, he switched to professionalism. "Have you seen a doctor? Are you having any discomfort, any side effects?"

"Yes, I've seen a doctor." She smiled again, soothed by

the objective questions. "No, I'm not having any discomfort, and after an unfortunate month of morning sickness, I haven't any side effects. We're disgustingly healthy."

"And the father?"

She laced her hands again. "I'm sure he's very healthy, too."

"Kasey." He cupped his hand over her fingers to stop their movement. "What are his plans about the baby? Obviously, you've decided to complete the pregnancy. You and the baby's father must have come to terms of some kind."

"No, we haven't come to terms of any kind." She looked at him directly, and some of the vulnerability seeped through. "I haven't told him."

"Haven't told him?" He was more shocked by this than anything else. It simply wasn't like her. "When do you plan to?"

"I plan not to." She reached for a cigarette and began to tear it into small pieces.

"Kasey, he has a right to know. It's his baby."

"No." Her eyes shot up again. "It's my baby. The baby has rights, I have rights. Jordan can take care of himself."

"That's not like you, Kasey," he said quietly.

"Please." She shook her head and crushed the remains of the cigarette in her hand. "Don't. I didn't make this decision overnight. I've thought about it for months. I know it's the right thing to do. My baby isn't going to be pulled apart because his father and I made mistakes. I know what would happen if I told Jordan."

Her voice was beginning to shake, and she took a moment to steady it. "He'd offer to marry me. He's an honorable man. I'd refuse because I couldn't bear . . ." Her voice broke again, and she shook her head impatiently. "I couldn't bear to have him ask me out of obligation. Then he'd want to set me up some kind of financial support. I don't need it. My baby doesn't need it. There'd have to be structured visitation rights with the baby bouncing from coast to coast, never knowing where he belonged. It's not fair. I won't have it. The baby belongs to me."

He took her hands again and gave her a long look. "Do you love the father?"

He watched her crumple before his eyes. "Oh, God, yes." Kasey laid her head on the table and wept.

Her grandfather let her cry it out. He hadn't seen this sort of grief from her since she had been a child. He kept her hands in his and waited. What sort of man was this Jordan, whose baby she carried? If she loved him, why was she weeping here alone instead of sharing the joy of impending parenthood with him?

He tried to remember the patches of information from her letters. He knew who Jordan was—the writer she had worked with during late fall and early winter of the last year. Dr. Brennan had admired his work. Kasey's letters had been enthusiastic and confusing. But he was used to both from her.

Why hadn't he read between the lines? And now, for months, she had been dealing with the most important decision in her life alone. He hated to see her this way—lost, weeping. Once he had had to send her away from him. She had been lost and weeping then, too. He had thought his own decision had been right for her, and when the dust had settled, it had been. But the time in between had had its effect on her. He was intuitive enough to know that part of her present decision stemmed from her own experiences. All he could offer her was time and support and his love. He hoped it would be enough.

Her weeping had stopped. Kasey kept her head down on the table while she rested from it. She hadn't given in to tears for months. Slowly she straightened and began to speak again.

"I loved him—I do love him. That's one of the reasons I'm handling it this way." She sighed. She had needed to talk to someone since she had walked out of Beatrice's sitting room four months before. "Let me explain things to you, and maybe you'll understand."

Her voice was quiet now, without emotion, and she

detailed the circumstances in the Taylor household. When she spoke of Alison, he saw the parallel immediately and kept his silence. Only when she told him of her final encounter with Beatrice did he explode.

"Are you telling me she threatened you?" He had sprung up, forgetting the strain in his back. He was ready to fight.

"Not me." Kasey reached for his hand and drew herself to her feet. "Jordan, Alison. There was nothing she could do to me, nothing that would have mattered."

"It was blackmail, Kasey. Simple, ugly blackmail." His voice was rough with temper. "You should have gone straight to Jordan and told him."

"Do you know what he would have done?" Kasey took his arm. "He would have stormed in there, just as you'd like to do right now. It would have been a horrible scene with Alison right in the middle of it. Do you think I could take a chance on there being a court battle? She's just a little girl. I know how she'd feel seeing her name and picture splashed in the papers, listening to the whispering." Her eyes were eloquent, and her tears had dried. "Put yourself in my place, Pop. You were very close to it once. If you had to change what you did all those years ago, would you?"

He sighed and drew her into his arms. "Kasey, I never thought you'd have to go through something like this again."

She had needed to come home, to feel his big, strong arms and gentle hands. She had needed a rock and had never known a sturdier one. "I love you, Pop."

"I love you, Kasey." He held her for a moment and said nothing. It struck him suddenly that she was no longer willow slim. He could feel the roundness as she pressed against him. Unprofessionally, he was shocked by the change. She wasn't his baby anymore but a woman carrying one of her own. "It just occurs to me," he said softly. "I'm going to be a great-grandfather."

"You've always been a great grandfather," Kasey murmured. "The best."

"You'll stay until the baby comes."

Kasey sighed and relaxed against him. "I'll stay."

He drew her away. "Are you taking vitamins?"

"Yes, Doctor." She grinned and kissed his cheek.

"And drinking your milk?"

She kissed his other cheek. "What do you think of Bryan?" she asked him. "It could work whether the baby's a boy or a girl. I think Bryan Wyatt has a nice sound. Dignified but not stuffy."

He lifted his brows. "I can see my work's cut out for me."

"Or there's Paul," she went on as he walked to the refrigerator. "Of course, I'd have to have a boy, then." Kasey watched as he poured a tall glass of milk. "Are we going to have some of Mrs. Oates's goodies now?" She opened the bundle. "Are these damson preserves?" she asked as she held up a Mason jar. "I love damson preserves."

"Good." Dr. Brennan handed her the glass of milk and smiled. "You can have some with your milk before I examine you."

CHAPTER FIFTEEN

I T WAS JULY BEFORE KASEY KNEW IT. THERE WERE WILD-flowers in the woods and geraniums in the kitchen window box. At night the crickets sang incessantly. She could lie in bed late and listen to them while the baby moved restlessly inside her. He's in a hurry, she thought. Or they are. Her grandfather was all but certain there were two. She had refused his suggestion that they go down to the hospital and make certain. She wanted to be surprised.

It had been a long time since she had slept deeply. The baby wouldn't permit it. *They* wouldn't permit it. Kasey didn't need any sophisticated equipment to tell her there were two. No one baby could be so active. When one slept, the other was wide-awake and kicking. And she was huge.

Kasey rested a hand on either side of her stomach. I won't go full term, she mused. Twins traditionally arrive early. Closing her eyes, she began to drift again. She liked the movements inside her, liked knowing life was growing, impatient to arrive. She could almost see how they would look. A boy and a girl, she thought, with warm brown hair and dark blue eyes. When she looked at the eyes, she would think of Jordan.

She shifted again as she felt the distinct shove of an elbow. What was he doing now? she wondered. What time was it in California? Early enough that he might still be working? Would he have finished the book? Kasey wanted badly to find it in a bookstore, to bring it home and closet herself with it. It would bring him back, along with all the hours they had spent together in his study. She could save it for her children. They would never know it was their father who had written it, but they would learn to admire and respect him through his words. She wanted that for them and for Jordan.

And Alison. Kasey rolled from her side to her back. She had written the girl, as she had promised. Her own zigzagging course across the country had made it impossible for Alison to answer. I should hear from her soon now, Kasey mused. I've been settled for nearly two months. I wrote nearly three weeks ago.

Kasey pulled herself from bed and walked to the window. It was hot and sultry, making sleep that much more difficult. It might be best if she did forget me. I can hardly ask her to visit me now. She stroked her hand over her stomach. There'd be no way to explain to her and no way to be certain Jordan wouldn't find out. He'll take care of her and keep her safe. And I'll do the same for our babies.

The movement inside her stopped. Kasey went back to bed and slept.

DR. BRENNAN WATCHED KASEY AS SHE KNELT ON THE ground between rows of vegetables and weeded. She was blooming. He had no worries about her physically. She was the picture of health, and strong. She had taken up her life again with characteristic enthusiasm. He was proud of her.

He had some doubts about the wisdom of her decision, but she was dead certain. He had plans to speak with her again about Jordan, but he would give her until she had delivered and was on her feet again. The baby was his main concern. And the baby's mother.

"I don't know why I planted lima beans," she muttered and ripped at a stubborn weed. "I hate lima beans, but I just love the way they all sit in a fat little pod. I suppose I could have them bronzed." She sat back on her heels and dusted her hands. "Some of the tomatoes are ripe. You could have them with supper tonight with the corn Lloyd Cramer gave you for his appendix." She shielded her eyes from the sun and smiled up at him.

"I got the best of the deal. His appendix was in bad shape."

"You're so mercenary." She held up a hand so he could help her to her feet, then she kissed him with her usual exuberance. "Do you think I should water the garden? It hasn't rained all week."

He glanced up at the sky. "Watering the garden's a sure way to bring it on. We could use it. The heat's keeping you up at night."

"That, among other things." She patted her stomach. "And, no, I'm not tired." She laughed, anticipating his question. "I've got enough energy for all of us."

"Did you have your milk today?"

"My carrots aren't doing well," Kasey responded. "I'm going to get the hose."

"I'll water it this evening when it cools off. Go have a glass now."

"I'll throw up," she threatened.

"That hasn't worked since you were twelve."

She narrowed her eyes, measuring him. She knew he was every bit as stubborn as she was. "I'm going to make scalloped potatoes for dinner. And vanilla custard. That's enough milk for anybody."

"You'll get fat."

"I *am* fat." She dashed into the house before he could comment.

She sat at the kitchen table and peeled. A small mountain of potatoes was growing in front of her. There was something soothing in the simple, mindless chore, and she skinned more than her grandfather and she could possibly eat in a single sitting. We'll have leftovers, she decided and glanced at the pile. All week. This is the last one, she promised herself and shook the potato in her hand. Or we'll have to invite the neighborhood. She didn't glance up as the door opened but continued wielding the peeler. "You might have to dig up a couple of starving patients," she said aloud. "I got carried away here. You know, they don't peel potatoes by hand in the army anymore, a terrible lack of tradition. They have these machines, and . . ."

She glanced up and froze.

Jordan watched the color drain slowly from her face. He saw vivid shock in her eyes, and fear. The fear made his stomach twist. She dropped the peeler, and her hands shot under the table.

Oh, God, dear God, she thought desperately. What do I do? What do I say?

He said nothing, but his eyes were riveted on her face. Her hair was longer, he noted, almost to her shoulders now. When had she grown beautiful? She had been striking, alluring, unforgettable. But when had she grown beautiful? He couldn't take his eyes from her face. How long had he waited to see it again, to watch it light up for him? It wasn't lit now; it was terrified. That was his doing, but it wasn't too late. It couldn't be too late. All these months of desperation couldn't be for nothing.

Was her skin as soft as he remembered? Would she cringe if he touched her? He was afraid to test it and could only stare at her.

Kasey gripped her hands together tightly under the table. She had to do something, to say something. She waited a moment until she was certain her voice wouldn't give her away.

"Hello, Jordan." She smiled at him while her nails bit into her palms. "Passing through?"

He took a few steps toward her but kept the table between them. Without it he would have to touch her. "I've been looking for you for months." It came out as an accusation. He hadn't meant to greet her that way. He had sworn to himself he would be calm, but calmness had deserted him the moment she had looked up at him.

"Have you?" Kasey managed to keep her eyes level. "I'm

sorry. I've been doing some traveling. Is it something about the book? I don't know of anything we didn't cover."

"Would you stop!" He was shouting at her. How could he be shouting at her now? he asked himself. But he couldn't stop. Everything that had kept him going since she had left had crumbled the moment he had set eyes on her again. "I've spent six months in hell. How can you sit there looking at me as though I were a neighbor dropping in for a visit?" He skirted the table before she could speak and dragged her to her feet. "Damn it, Kasey . . ." His voice trailed off as he looked at her. "Oh, God." It was barely more than a whisper as his gaze swept down, then up to her face again. "You're pregnant."

"Yes, I am." His hold had loosened. She felt his fingers drop away one at a time. He stared at her as though he'd never seen her before.

"You . . ." He shook his head as if he were resurfacing. "You're carrying my child, and you haven't told me."

She took a step away from him. "My child, Jordan. I never said it was yours."

She was pulled back against him so quickly, she didn't have time to gasp. His eyes were no longer blank, but furious. "Look at me," he demanded between his teeth. "Look at me and say it's not mine." He saw the fear jump into her eyes again and released her. Why couldn't he stop himself from repeating the mistake that had caused him to lose her? Jordan turned away and searched for control. He hadn't been prepared for this. How could he have been prepared for this? A long, long moment passed before he could trust himself to speak again.

"In God's name, Kasey," he said quietly. "How could you keep this from me? No matter how you felt about me, I had a right to know."

"My baby has rights, Jordan." Her voice held the deadly calm of desperation. "I'm not concerned with yours."

He faced her again, ready to plead if necessary. He'd shelved his pride months before. "Don't shut me out, Kasey, please." He started to touch her, then, when she stiffened, he dropped his hand to his side. There were a hundred things he had planned to say when he finally found her, but now there was only one. "I love you."

"No!" She struck out at him in a furious slap. "Don't you say that to me! Don't you dare say that to me now." Her eyes were dry one minute and flooding the next. "I would have given anything to have heard that from you six months ago. *Anything.* What you gave me was a note and a check for services rendered, as though I were a—"

"No, Kasey. Please, you can't think . . ." He reached for her again, but she pushed him away.

"I haven't slept with many men. Surprised?" She drew

both hands over her cheeks to push away tears. "But you're the first who ever left payment."

"Kasey, no, it was nothing like that." Her words left him shaken. "Let me explain."

"I don't want explanations." She shook her head and walked away from him. "I want you to go. I asked you once before to leave me alone. Now I'm asking you again."

"I couldn't then, I can't now. Don't you understand?"

"I don't want to understand." She took deep breaths. "I don't need to." Her voice was calm again, but she didn't turn to him. "I'm sorry I hit you. I've never done anything like that before."

"Kasey, please." Gently he touched her shoulder. "Just sit down and listen to me. You loved me once. I can't leave this way." She didn't move. She didn't answer. Jordan felt the panic rising up and forced it down again. "Just hear me out, then I'll go if that's what you want."

"All right." She moved away from his touch and sat down. "I'll listen to you."

He didn't know where to begin or how. Where were his words? "When I woke up that last morning . . ." He hesitated. His mind was so crowded with all he wanted to say, and his emotions were hammering at him. She carried his child inside her. Right now she had her hands folded over her stomach as if she would protect what was partly his from him.

"When I woke up," he continued, "I hated myself. I remembered that I had come into your room. I remembered everything I had said to you, what I had done. You were still sleeping. I left the note because I thought you wouldn't want to see me again."

"Why did you think that?"

"Dear God, Kasey, I . . ." He had had to deal with it for half a year, and now he had to say it. "I raped you. I woke up and there were bruises on your arms that I had put there." Now it was he who turned away. He walked to a window, and his knuckles whitened on the sill. "I'll have to live with that for my entire life."

Kasey sat in silence for a moment. An honorable man, she thought and laid her hands on the arms of the chair. And an honorable man can't bear knowing he could contemplate doing something dishonorable. Perhaps if she hadn't hurt so badly herself, she could have read his pain in the note he had left her.

"Jordan." She waited until he turned to face her again. "What happened that night was a long way from rape. I could have stopped you or fought you all the way. You know I didn't."

"It wouldn't have made any difference if you had." He walked to her again. "I was drunk and crazy. I hurt you. You told me from the very beginning I would." He paused again but never took his eyes from her face. "I think you should know that I was going to ask you to marry me that night." He saw the shock fill her eyes before they closed.

"When I got back from seeing Harry and found you'd gone, I couldn't believe it. I got angry quickly; it was easier to deal with that way. You opened me up, forced me to feel again, and then when you meant everything to me, you walked away. I wanted to hurt you."

She still sat with her eyes closed, and he studied her face as he spoke. "For weeks, those first weeks after you walked into my life, I had told myself I couldn't be in love with you. It was too quick. I was just attracted, intrigued. If I hadn't been such a fool, I might not have lost you. You gave me everything freely, and I took it, but I was afraid to give too much back to you."

She opened up her eyes again and looked at him. "There's too much in the way even now, Jordan. Please don't say any more."

"You told me you'd listen. You're going to hear it all." He watched her hands slip back over the baby. Something ripped inside him, and he took a moment before continuing.

"After that last night together, when you'd gone, I tried to forget. I told myself you'd lied to me. I told myself you'd been playing a game. Then I'd remember how you looked that first time you told me you loved me. I knew you had gone because I hadn't given you anything back and because when I'd had my last chance, I'd hurt you."

"Jordan, it's done," she began. "Don't—"

"I tried to live without you." He shook his head and crouched down in front of her chair so their eyes were nearly level. "There was no color. You'd taken all the color with you. I came after you."

"Came after me?" she repeated.

"Your first letter to Alison came from Montana. When I got there, you'd left three days before. Three days. It might as well have been years. You'd left no forwarding address. And because you'd rented a car, there was no way of tracing you. I started to hire detectives, but then I remembered." He stopped again and rose. "I thought how you might feel. So instead, I went back and prayed for you to write Alison again."

Jordan dragged a hand through his hair as he relived the frustration and panic. "Each time you wrote, I tried to catch you before you moved on. Once, I missed you by five hours. I thought I'd go mad. I knew I couldn't keep leaving Alison that way, even for a day or two. And I began to think you'd keep moving, one step ahead of me, for the rest of my life. Then your last letter came.

"When you said you were going to be staying with your grandfather for a few months, Alison was so excited. Losing you has been hard on her."

Kasey shook her head and balled her hands into fists. "Don't."

"I'm sorry." He took one of her rigid hands into his. "As soon as she got the letter, she wanted to come out and see you. She said you told her she could."

"Yes, I had." Kasey removed her hand. She couldn't let him touch her, not now. She'd never be strong enough to send him away if he was touching her.

Jordan looked down at his empty hand a moment, then slipped it into his pocket. "I didn't want to leave her with my mother again, not even for a few days. I told her we'd both come."

"Alison's here?" Kasey felt the smile light her face. "Outside?"

"No." Jordan swallowed the envy. The smile was for Alison, but not for him. "I wanted to see you alone first. Had to see you alone. She's back at the hotel. There's a family there with a couple of kids who've taken to her. She was hoping you'd come with me when I went back to get her."

Kasey shook her head. "I can't do that. I'd love to see her if you'd bring her here."

Jordan felt a fresh flash of pain. He was losing and he was powerless to prevent it. "All right, if that's what you want. We're taking the rest of the summer to look for a new place."

"A new place?"

He had to talk about something, anything, to keep from pressuring her. To keep from begging her. "I decided some time ago, just before Christmas, actually, that Alison needed to get out of that house, away from my mother. I've already had the papers drawn up to turn the house over to her. We won't need anything so large. I told Alison we'd look together and try to be settled somewhere by the time she starts school again."

He was ready to explode. Jordan turned to her again, and the passion showed in his face. "Don't ask me to leave now that I've found you, Kasey. Don't turn away from me. You can't ask me to walk away from you, from my child."

"My child." Kasey rose now. She'd be stronger if she were standing.

"Our child," Jordan corrected quietly. "You can't change that. A child's entitled to know his father. If you can't think of me, think of the baby."

"I am thinking of the baby." She pressed her hands to her temples and pushed. Maybe it would ease the tension. "I didn't expect you to come here; I didn't expect you to love me. I knew what I had to do."

"But I did come." Jordan took her shoulders gently. "And I do love you."

"No." She stepped back, shaking her head. "Don't touch me."

She covered her eyes and didn't see the flash of emotion in Jordan's. "I knew what I had to do," she repeated. "I can't afford to think about you, about me. I have to think of my baby. I can't take chances with my baby."

"Chances?" Jordan began, but she was stumbling on.

"I won't have him shipped from coast to coast. He's going to know where he belongs. Nobody's going to pull at him. I won't have it. Not this time; this time it's my choice." She was sobbing now with her hands covering her face. He knew no way to bring comfort. "This is my baby, not a piece of property we can split down the middle. She might try to get at me through the baby. She might try to take him from me. I lost you, I lost Alison, but I can't lose this baby. It would kill me. Your mother's not going to get her hands on my baby!"

"What are you talking about?" He forgot himself and took her elbows, pulling her hands from her eyes. "What are you saying?"

Kasey didn't answer. She was breathing quickly. She didn't know what she had said.

Jordan's eyes narrowed to slits. "Did my mother have anything to do with your leaving?" Kasey started to shake her head, but his look stopped her. "You don't lie worth a damn, so don't try it. What did she say to you? What did she do?" When she didn't answer, he forced his voice into calmness. There was fear in her eyes again, but this time he knew it wasn't he who had put it there. "You're going to tell me exactly what went on between you."

"A very good idea." Dr. Brennan spoke as he came in the front door. Jordan glanced over but didn't release Kasey's arms. No one was going to stop him from learning the truth now. "No need to pick up the club, son," he told Jordan, amused. "I told her that's what she should do when she came home months ago."

"Pop, don't interfere."

"Don't interfere." He raised his brows at his granddaughter. "You always were snippy."

"Pop, please." Kasey pulled her arms away from Jordan. "You've got to stay out of this."

"The devil I do!" he boomed out at her. "This man has a right to know what went on behind his back. You just stopped playing solitaire, Kasey. I've dealt him in."

She shook her head, going to him. "Alison."

"He'll take care of Alison, Kasey. Any fool could see that. Are you going to tell him, or am I?"

"You tell me," Jordan addressed Dr. Brennan directly. "I want it straight."

"Sensible. Sit down and shut up, Kasey," her grandfather ordered.

"No, I won't—"

"Kathleen, *sit*!"

Her chin came up at the tone, but the training of a lifetime had her obeying.

"All right, Jordan," the doctor began. "This might not be easy to hear. Would you like to sit down?"

"No." Jordan bit off the word, then caught himself. "No, thank you."

"I will, I'm getting old." Dr. Brennan settled himself. "Your mother put Kasey in a position of choosing," he began. "I would conclude that she's an excellent judge of character, as she must have known what Kasey's choice would be. Her own happiness, or yours and Alison's."

"I don't understand what you're saying."

"The best way is straight up, then. Your mother threatened to sue for custody of Alison unless Kasey took her bags and left on the spot."

"Sue for . . ." Jordan pulled his hand through his hair again. "That's crazy. She doesn't want Alison, and in any case, there wouldn't be grounds for a suit."

"I said she was a good judge of character." Dr. Brennan glanced at his granddaughter. Frowning, Jordan followed his eyes. He felt the strength drain out of him.

"Oh, God." He rubbed his hands over his face in a gesture of fatigue. "I suppose she found out about Kasey's background. She should have come to me." He spoke quietly to the doctor again. "I would never have let my mother get away with a threat like that. She should have come to me."

"Yes." Dr. Brennan nodded in agreement. "But she wouldn't take the risk with two people she loved. Your mother threatened to sue on grounds of immoral conduct."

"Pop." The word was only a tired whisper.

"All of it, Kasey, all at once. And"—he turned back to Jordan—"she offered to pay her. That was her only miscalculation."

There was a window above the kitchen sink that looked out over the mountains. Jordan walked to it and stared out. "I'm having a difficult time handling this." His voice was strained and raw. "I knew she was capable of a lot of things, but I wouldn't have believed this of her. I appreciate your telling me." Jordan thought he had felt all the rage he could feel, all the pain he could stand. But he'd been wrong. Now he wasn't sure which was uppermost. "I'll deal with my mother, Dr. Brennan, you can be sure of it."

"I am sure of it." After casting a last look at Kasey, her grandfather rose. "I have a garden to water." He left them, and the room dropped into silence.

Kasey took a deep breath. It was out now, all of it. There would be little more to say. "I'm going to fix some tea." Rising, she walked over to set a kettle on to boil.

"Kasey, there's nothing I can say or do that will ever make up for this."

"It wasn't your doing, Jordan, and it's not your place to make up for it." She reached above her head into a cupboard. "It's herbal tea. Pop's cut off my caffeine."

"Kasey, please, keep still a minute." She stopped and turned to face him. Jordan drew together all of his words. He had to say everything quickly and get it out while he could still stand. "First, I promise you, my mother will never come anywhere near our—your baby." He felt the pain rolling around in his stomach as he relinquished his rights. "I won't make any demands. I'll give you financial support if you'll take it. I'll understand if you won't."

"Jordan—"

"No, don't say anything yet." He knew he had to get it

out quickly. "The baby's yours, completely yours; I accept that. You have my word I won't ever make any claim. I know how much Alison means to you. I'll leave her with you for a few days if you like while I go back to deal with my mother."

"It doesn't matter, Jordan—"

"It matters to me!" He lifted a hand as if to stop himself from breaking free of control. "When I've found a place for us, and we're settled, I'll send your grandfather our address. All I'd like is to know when the baby comes and that you're all right."

His words were changing everything. What had made sense an hour before seemed absurd now. People who love should be together. "Jordan," she began, then made a slight sound and pressed a hand to her side.

"What is it?" Panicked, he grabbed her arms. "Are you in pain? Is it the baby? Oh, God, I should never have come. I should never have upset you this way. I'll call your grandfather."

"That's not necessary." Kasey smiled at him. "The baby's kicking, that's all. He's very active."

Jordan looked down. Slowly he brought up his hand to place his palm on the mound of her stomach. Life quivered impatiently beneath it. Simple wonder flooded through him. Part of himself was growing in there. Part of Kasey. Between them, they'd created a human being. He could almost feel the outline of a tiny foot as it pounded against his hand.

When he lifted his eyes to hers, Kasey saw the swimming emotion, the dazed awe. She smiled and laid her hand on top of his. "You should feel it when he really gets going."

The pain swept down on him immediately, stealing his color. That would be his first and last contact with his child. The last time he touched the woman he loved. Kasey saw the change before he turned to walk to the door.

Don't let him go, her heart shouted at her. Don't be a fool. *It's a risk,* her mind reminded her. For you, for all of you. *Take the risk,* her heart insisted. You're strong enough. You're all strong enough.

"Jordan." She called to him before he reached the door. "Don't go." When he turned, she was halfway across the room. "We need you." She threw her arms around his neck. "I need you."

He wanted to take what she offered but held himself back. "Kasey, you don't have to do this for me. I don't want . . ."

"Oh, shut up and kiss me. There's been too much talk. It's been so long." She found his mouth, then heard his quiet moan of relief.

"I love you." He rained kisses over her face. "You'll never go a day without hearing me say that again. I love you."

"Really kiss me," she murmured, trying to halt his roving mouth. "You won't break the babies."

He pulled her against him, losing himself in her taste. She was his—finally, completely his. "Babies?" he said suddenly and drew her away. *"Babies?"*

"Didn't I mention there were two?"

Jordan shook his head and gave a quick, astonished laugh. "No." He laughed again and crushed her against him. He could feel the lives inside her shifting and stretching. "No, you didn't mention it. How did I live without you for more than half a year? It wasn't living." He answered his own question. "I've just started to live again." He gave her a feverish kiss as though he could fill six months of emptiness with one embrace. He drew her back again, and his eyes were intense. "Strings this time," he told her. "I want strings this time, Kasey."

"On both of us," she agreed and went into his arms.

EPILOGUE

THE FIRE ROARING IN THE HEARTH HAD THE LIVING room cozy with heat. Outside there was two feet of snow, and it was still falling. Kasey slipped a last-minute present under the Christmas tree, then stood back to admire it. Strings of popcorn draped and crisscrossed from top to bottom. She grinned, remembering the chaos of the kitchen the evening they had made them. Chaos remained one of her favorite things.

Bending, she toyed with a box with her name on the tag.

"Cheating?" Jordan asked from the doorway, and she quickly straightened.

"Certainly not." She waited until he had crossed the

room and slipped his arms around her. "Just poking. Poking's not cheating. Poking's required at Christmas."

"Is that your educated analysis, Dr. Taylor?" He nuzzled into her neck, finding his favorite spot.

"Absolutely. How's the book coming?"

"Fine. I have a fascinating main character." He drew her away to look at her. She was glowing. Was it Christmas Eve that made her glow this way? "I love you, Kasey." He kissed her gently. "And I'm proud of you."

"What for?" She linked her hands behind his neck and smiled. "I like specific compliments."

"For earning your doctorate, raising a family, making a home."

"Of course, I did it all by myself." Smiling, she cupped his face in her hands. "Jordan, you're terribly sweet. I'm crazy about you." She drew him close until their mouths met.

It took only an instant for the kiss to heat. They were locked tight, enveloped in each other. Soft pleasure and hot passion merged.

"It's snowing," Jordan murmured.

"I noticed." Kasey sighed softly as his lips brushed her neck.

"We've got plenty of wood."

"You chop it beautifully. I'm always impressed." She

drew his head back far enough so that her mouth could find his.

"There's wine in the cellar." Desire was pushing at him. The wanting never seemed to lessen. He slipped his hand under her shirt to roam her back. "Do you remember the fantasy we talked about on Christmas Eve two years ago?"

"Mmm." Kasey pressed closer. "Snowed in," she murmured. "With wood and wine and each other."

The cocker spaniel came barreling into the room just ahead of two scrambling toddlers.

Run for your life, Kasey thought, smiling as she rested her head on Jordan's shoulder.

"Bryan, Paul, you two come back here." Alison bounded into the room on their heels. "You know you're not supposed to tease Maxwell." She sighed and shook her head as the twins collapsed on the floor with the dog clutched between them.

Jordan watched as his children noisily adored the long-suffering dog. He slipped his arm more snugly around Kasey's shoulders. "They're gorgeous," he murmured. "It always astonishes me how perfectly gorgeous they are."

"And so well-mannered," Kasey observed as Bryan shoved Paul aside to ensure a better grip on the dog's neck. Alison dove in to referee.

He laughed and drew her to face him again. "About that fantasy . . ."

"I'll meet you at midnight," she whispered. "Right here."

"You bring the wine, I'll bring the wood."

"It's a deal." The children grew noisier, and Kasey knew a private conversation would soon be impossible. Besides, she wanted to get down and play, too. "One more thing," she added and gave him one of her guileless smiles.

He gave her a puzzled look, and she brought her mouth close to his. "We're going to have another baby," she told him. "Or two," she managed before his mouth crushed hers.

Keep reading for an excerpt from the final book
in the Cousins O'Dwyer Trilogy by Nora Roberts

BLOOD MAGICK

Now available from Berkley Books

Winter 2013

BRANNA O'DWYER WOKE TO A GRAY, SOGGY, relentless rain. And wished for nothing more than to burrow in and sleep again. Mornings, she had always felt, came forever too soon. But like it or not, sleep was done, and with its leaving came a slow and steady craving for coffee.

Annoyed, as she was often annoyed by morning, she rose, pulled thick socks over her feet, drew a sweater over the thin T-shirt she'd slept in.

Through habit and an ingrained tidiness, she stirred up the bedroom fire so the licks of flame would cheer the room, and with her hound, Kathel, having his morning stretch on the hearthrug, she made her bed, added the mounds of pretty pillows that pleased her.

In her bath, she brushed out her long fall of black hair, then bundled it up. She had work, and plenty of it—after coffee. She frowned at herself in the mirror, considered doing a bit of a glamour, as the restless night surely showed. But didn't see the point.

Instead, she walked back into the bedroom, gave Kathel a good rub to get his tail wagging.

"You were restless as well, weren't you now? I heard you talking in your sleep. Did you hear the voices, my boy?"

They walked down together, quiet, as her house was full as it was too often these days. Her brother and Meara shared his bed, and her cousin Iona shared hers with Boyle.

Friends and family all. She loved them, and needed them. But God be sweet, she could've done with some alone.

"They stay for me," she told Kathel as they walked down the steps of the pretty cottage. "As if I can't look after myself. Have I not put enough protection around what's mine, and theirs, to hold off a dozen Cabhans?"

It had to stop, really, she decided, heading straight toward her lovely, lovely coffee machine. A man of Boyle McGrath's size could hardly be comfortable in her cousin Iona's little bed. She needed to nudge them along. In any case, there had been no sign nor shadow of Cabhan since Samhain.

"We almost had him. Bugger it, we nearly finished it."

The spell, the potion, both so strong, she thought as she started the coffee. Hadn't they worked on both hard and long? And the power, by the gods, the power had risen like a flood that night by Sorcha's old cabin.

They'd hurt him, spilled his blood, sent him howling—wolf and man. And still . . .

Not done. He'd slipped through, and would be healing, would be gathering himself.

Not done, and at times she wondered if ever it would be.

She opened the door, and Kathel rushed out. Rain or no, the dog wanted his morning run. She stood in the open doorway, in the cold, frosty December air, looking toward the woods.

He waited, she knew, beyond them. In this time or in another, she couldn't tell. But he would come again, and they must be ready.

But he wouldn't come this morning.

She closed the door on the cold, stirred up the kitchen fire, added fuel so the scent of peat soothed. Pouring her coffee, she savored the first taste, and the short time of quiet and alone. And, a magick of its own, the coffee cleared her head, smoothed her mood.

We will prevail.

———

The voices, she remembered now. So many voices rising up, echoing out. Light and power and purpose. In sleep she'd felt it all. And that single voice, so clear, so sure.

We will prevail.

"We'll pray you're right about it."

She turned.

The woman stood, a hand protectively over the mound of her belly, a thick shawl tied around a long dress of dark blue.

Almost a mirror, Branna thought, almost like peering into a glass. The hair, the eyes, the shape of the face.

"You're Brannaugh of Sorcha. I know you from dreams."

"Aye, and you, Branna of the clan O'Dwyer. I know you from dreams. You're my blood."

"I am. I am of the three." Branna touched the amulet with its icon of the hound she was never without—just as her counterpart did the same.

"Your brother came to us, with his woman, one night in Clare."

"Connor, and Meara. She is a sister to me." Now Branna touched her heart. "Here. You understand."

"She saved my own brother from harm, shed blood for him. She is a sister to me as well." With some wonder on her face, Sorcha's Brannaugh looked around the kitchen. "What is this place?"

"My home. And yours for you are very welcome here. Will you sit? I would make you tea. This coffee I have would not be good for the baby."

"It has a lovely scent. But only sit with me, cousin. Just sit for a moment. This is a wondrous place."

Branna looked around her kitchen—tidy, lovely, as she'd designed it herself. And, she supposed, wondrous indeed to a woman from the thirteenth century.

"Progress," she said as she sat at the kitchen table with her cousin. "It eases hours of work. Are you well?"

"I am, very well. My son comes soon. My third child." She reached out; Branna took her hand.

Heat and light, a merging of power very strong, very true.

"You will name him Ruarc, for he will be a champion."

It brought a smile to her cousin's face. "So I will."

"On Samhain, we—the three and three more who are with us—battled Cabhan. Though we caused him harm, burned and bled him, we didn't finish him. I saw you there. Your brother with a sword, your sister with a wand, you with a bow. You were not with child."

"Samhain is yet a fortnight to come in my time. We came to you?"

"You did, at Sorcha's cabin where we lured him, and in

your time as we shifted into it to try to trap him. We were close, but it wasn't enough. My book—Sorcha's book—I could show you the spell, the poison we conjured. You may—"

Brannaugh held up a hand, pressed the other to her side. "My son comes. And he pulls me back. But listen, there is a place, a holy place. An abbey. It sits in a field, a day's travel south."

"Ballintubber. Iona weds her Boyle there come spring. It is a holy place, a strong place."

"He cannot go there, see there. It is sacred, and those who made us watch over it. They gave us, Sorcha's three, their light, their hope and strength. When next you face down Cabhan, we will be with you. We will find a way. We will prevail. If it is not to be you, there will come another three. Believe, Branna of the O'Dwyers. Find the way."

"I can do nothing else."

"Love." She gripped Branna's hand hard. "Love, I have learned, is another guide. Trust your guides. Oh, he's impatient. My child comes today. Be joyful, for he is another bright candle against the dark. Believe," she said again, and vanished.

Branna rose, and with a thought lit a candle for the new light, the new life.

And with a sigh, accepted her alone was at an end.

So she started breakfast. She had a story to tell, and no one would want to hear it on an empty stomach. Believe, she thought— Well, she believed it was part of her lot in life to cook for an army on nearly a daily basis.

She swore an oath that when they'd sent Cabhan to hell she'd take a holiday, somewhere warm, sunny—where she wouldn't touch a pot, pan, or skillet for days on end.

She began to mix the batter for pancakes—a recipe new to her she'd wanted to try—and Meara came in.

Her friend was dressed for the day, a working day at the stables, in thick trousers, a warm sweater, sturdy boots. She'd braided back her bark brown hair, sent Branna a cautious look with her dark gypsy eyes.

"I promised I'd see to breakfast this morning."

"I woke early, after a restless night. And have already had company this morning."

"Someone's here?"

"Was here. Drag the others down, would you, so I'll tell my tale all at once." She hesitated only a moment. "Best if Connor or Boyle rings up Fin, and asks if he'd come over as well."

"It's Cabhan. Is he back?"

"He's coming, right enough, but no."

"I'll get the others. Everyone's up, so it won't take long."

With a nod, Branna set bacon sizzling in a pan.

Connor came first, and her brother sniffed the air like Kathel might do.

"Be useful," she told him. "Set the table."

"Straightaway. Meara said something happened, but it wasn't Cabhan."

"Do you think I'd be trying my hand with these pancake things if I'd gone a round with Cabhan?"

"I don't." He fetched plates from the cupboard. "He stays in the shadows. He's stronger than he was, but not full healed. I barely feel him yet, but Fin said he's not full healed."

And Finbar Burke would know, Branna thought, as he was Cabhan's blood, as he bore the mark of Sorcha's curse.

"He's on his way," Connor added.

When she only nodded, he went to the door, opened it for Kathel. "And look at you, wet as a seal."

"Dry him off," Branna began, then sighed when Connor simply saw to the task by gliding his hands over the wet fur. "We've towels in the laundry for that."

Connor only grinned, a quick flash from a handsome face, a quick twinkle in moss green eyes. "Now he's dry all the faster, and you don't have a wet towel to wash."

Iona and Boyle came in, hand in hand. A pair of love-birds, Branna thought. If anyone had suggested to her a year before that the taciturn, often brusque, former brawler could resemble a lovebird she'd have laughed till her ribs cracked. But there he was, big, broad-shouldered, his hair tousled, his tawny eyes just a little dreamy beside her bright sprite of an American cousin.

"Meara will be right down," Iona announced. "She had a call from her sister."

"All's well?" Connor asked. "Her ma?"

"No problems—just some Christmas details." Without being asked she got out flatware to finish what Connor started, and Boyle put the kettle on for tea.

So Branna's kitchen filled with voices, with movement—and she could admit now that she'd had coffee—with the warmth of family. And then excitement as Meara dashed in, grabbed Connor and pulled him into a dance.

"I'm to pack up the rest of my mother's things." She did a quick stomp, click, stomp, then grabbed Connor again for a hard kiss. "She's staying with my sister Maureen for the duration. Praise be, and thanks to the little Baby Jesus in his manger!"

Even as Connor laughed, she stopped, pressed her hands to her face. "Oh God, I'm a terrible daughter, a horrible person altogether. Dancing about because my own mother's gone to live with my sister in Galway and I'll not have to deal with her on a daily basis myself."

"You're neither," Connor corrected. "Are you happy your mother's happy?"

"Of course, I am, but—"

"And why shouldn't you be? She's found a place where she's content, where she has grandchildren to spoil. And why shouldn't you kick up your heels a bit as she won't be ringing you up twice a day when she can't work out how to switch out a lightbulb?"

"Or burns another joint of lamb," Boyle added.

"That's the bloody truth, isn't it?" So Meara did another quick dance. "I'm happy for her, I am. And I'm wild with joy for my own self."

When Fin came in Meara launched herself at him—and gave Branna a moment to adjust herself, as she had to do whenever he walked in her door.

"You've lost a tenant, Finbar. My ma's settled once and done with my sister." She kissed him hard as well, made him laugh. "That's thanks to you—and don't say you don't need it—for the years of low rent, and for holding the little cottage in case she wanted to come back to Cong."

"She was a fine tenant. Kept the place tidy as a church."

"The place looks fine now, it does, with the updates we've done." As Iona took over the table setting, Connor grabbed his first coffee. "I expect Fin will have someone in there, quick as you please."

"I'll be looking into it." But it was Branna he looked at, and into. Then, saying nothing, took Connor's coffee for himself.

She kept her hands busy, and wished to bloody hell she'd done that little glamour. No restless night showed on his face, on that beautiful carving of it, in the bold green eyes.

He looked perfect—man and witch—with his raven black hair damp from the rain, his body tall and lean as he shed his black leather jacket, hung it on a peg.

She'd loved him all her life, understood, accepted, she always would. But the first and only time they'd given themselves to each other—so young, still so innocent—the mark had come on him.

Cabhan's mark.

A Dark Witch of Mayo could never be with Cabhan's blood.

She could, would, and had worked with him, for he'd proven time and again he wanted Cabhan's end as much as she. But there could never be more.

Did knowing it pained him as it did her help her through it? Maybe a bit, she admitted. Just a bit.

She took the platter heaped with pancakes she'd already flipped from the skillet out of the warmer, added the last of them.

"We'll sit then, and eat. It's your Nan's recipe, Iona. We'll see if I did her proud."

Even as she lifted the platter, Fin took it from her. And as he took it, his eyes met and held hers. "You've a story to go with them, I'm told."

"I do, yes." She took a plate full of bacon and sausage, carried it to the table. And sat. "Not an hour ago I sat here and had a conversation with Sorcha's Brannaugh."

"She came here?" Connor paused in the act of sliding a stack of pancakes onto his plate. "Our kitchen?"

"She did. I'd had a restless night, full of dreams and voices. Hers among them. I couldn't be sure of the place as it was vague and scattered as dreams can be." She took a single pancake for herself. "I was here, getting my first cup of coffee, and I turned around. There she was.

"She looks like me—or I like her. That was a jolt of surprise, just how close we are there—though she was heavily pregnant. Her son comes today—or not today, as in her time it was still a fortnight to Samhain."

"Time shifts," Iona murmured.

"As you say. They'd gone to Ballintubber Abbey on the way here. That's where the dream took me."

"Ballintubber." Iona shifted to Boyle. "I felt them there, remember? When you took me to see it, I felt them, knew they'd gone there. It's such a strong place."

"It is, yes," Branna agreed. "But I've been there more than once, as has Connor. I never felt them."

"You haven't been since Iona's come," Fin pointed out. "You haven't been there since the three are all in Mayo."

"True enough." And a good point, she was forced to admit. "But I will, we will. On your wedding day, Iona, if not before. She said the others, those before us, guard the place, so Cabhan's barred from it. He can't go in, see in. It's a true sanctuary if we find we need one. They, who came before, gave light and strength to the three. And hope—I think she needed that most."

"And you," Iona said, "all of us. Hope wouldn't hurt us either."

"I'm more for doing than hoping, but it gave her what she needed. I could see it. She said—in the dream, and here—we will prevail. To believe that, and they'll be with us when we face Cabhan again. To find the way. To know, if it isn't for us to finish, another three will come. We will prevail."